# THE NEXT
# GOD

a novel

## b.t. gottfred

# CONTENTS


Note from the Narrator ............ vii

Prelude ............ 1
1. First Contact ............ 3
2. The Love Interest ............ 12
3. The Road Trip, Part One ............ 24
   ***Notes app / Madison Pike / Nov 26 ............ 37
4. The Road Trip, Part Two ............ 40
5. The Wizard and the Court ............ 55
6. The Conversation ............ 66
7. The Motel, Part One ............ 82
   //////////////////// ............ 89
8. The Motel, Part Two ............ 91
9. The Silverado Confession ............ 95
10. The Last Coffee ............ 102
   ***Notes app / Madison Pike / Nov 27 ............ 111
11. Drinks & Thoughts ............ 114
12. The First (Magic) Act ............ 120
13. The Fear of What Might Be ............ 128
14. The Moments Before ............ 133
15. Portals ............ 144
   //////////////////// ............ 153
16. an Angry god ............ 154
17. The Moments After ............ 159
   //////////////////// ............ 167
18. Truths ............ 168
19. Travels ............ 174
20. Worlds ............ 186
21. Times ............ 193

/////////////////      197
THE END      200

Afterword      201

*Dedicated To*
*Our Fellow Searchers*

# NOTE FROM THE NARRATOR

*I don't know how to tell you everything,*
*but I promise to be honest about all*
*I see and feel.*

MY PARENTS TOOK me to get a puppy the day they told us they were getting divorced. At the shelter, I picked out a half-shepherd, half-chow. Black coat with a brown mane. She looked like she had lion blood. I named her Flame.

She died when I was twelve. Tumors no one knew were there until it was too late. The day Flame died was the day I stopped believing in God.

It was also the day I became obsessed with finding something new to believe in.

# FIRST CONTACT

> Think this is real?

A TEXT. From KC. A video link below. I ignored it. KC's an over-texter. Attempted to go back to sleep. It wasn't even 10 am yet.

> Cyur! Wake up and watch it!

My fingers were seconds from turning off notifications, when:

> Don't ignore me please!

> Watch the video tell me it's fake and then I'll let you go back to being a boring monk corpse

KC's my ex-girlfriend. We dated in high school.

She dumped me in the spring of our senior year. For a lot of reasons, but one was, "*Cyur, nothing seems real when we're together.*" Six months into college, she wanted to get back together. I told her something had changed for me. She yelled. A lot. I ignored every call and text for a month. Then for the past year, I'd only text back when she sent me videos of a certain curiosity.

> WATCH IT CYUR. This guy definitely is different than the rest. I swear.

Since I only responded when KC sent me videos of my very specific interest, she sent me lots of videos that she pretended could be authentic but were just veiled attempts to get back in my life.

> If you don't watch it, I'm getting in a car, driving a thousand miles to show it to you in person. Don't think your blonde rich girlfriend Madison is ready to meet me.

> You know what I mean.

Never knew when KC would cross a line. So I broke, texted back:

> Fine. Watching now.

> But no more threats or I'm gonna block you.

I scrolled up, clicked on the video from an account named "Shepherd":

IT'S a close up of his face. White guy. Older than me, but not old. Maybe late twenties. Blue eyes that knew their worth. Clean shaven and handsome. A face sculpted to sell razor blades. "Hello my beautiful souls," he said through a smile impossible not to like, "here is a small moment of magic to help you through your day." He took a step back, raised into the camera's view a small potted plant holding a wilted daffodil. Pinching two fingers around the stem, he focused his eyes on the dead flower. For almost two minutes, nothing happened. Then, slowly, bright green life crept from where his fingers touched to the rest of the flower. At seven minutes and twenty-six seconds, the daffodil fully bloomed and he let go. Sweating, out of breath. As if he had just sprinted ten miles on a hot summer day. He ended the video with, "You, too, are ready for a re-birth. And I am here as your witness, as your friend, and, if you so desire, as your Shepherd."

This 'trick' had been done in movies for a hundred years. Bringing a flower back to bloom was always a quick way to make the audience believe something otherworldly was at play. But two things made me want to watch more of his videos. One, that this act had exhausted him. Most practical and video magicians go to great lengths to make their act appear effortless. Second was the length. With our modern day attention span, most social media video apps are designed to award creators that give their viewers instant gratification. If not, they are swiped away into the virtual trash heap of the app's algorithm. But Shepherd's video started with two minutes of nothing. Followed by more than five glacial paced minutes until the daffodil was returned to full life. Ninety-nine percent of viewers would have swiped to another video — animals fighting, skydivers leaping, people naked-ing. And even ninety-nine percent of that last one percent would have gotten to the end and thought, *Seven minutes for that?*

For you to believe what Shepherd did was real you would have to really, *really* want to believe magic was real.

And I really, really, *really* did.

THERE WERE seven other videos on his page. Three levitations, including a small child hovering a meter above the sidewalk, whose wonder was either real or Oscar worthy. There was another flower rejuvenation. This time a rose. Twenty-three minutes long. Even I fast forwarded through it. The fifth video he seemed to scoop a ball of light out of the air in front of him. It had the most views but none of the comments talked about where he was scooping the light from. The sixth video he walked through a wall. The least views, with two edits inside the video that made it easy to dismiss as fake. But when he approached the camera at the end, to sign off with his usual *"...and I am here as your witness, as your friend, and, if you so desire, as your Shepherd"* I noticed a wood splinter in his ear, a drop of blood sprouting. A piece of the wall? Again, a tiny detail only for those of us who wanted to believe this was real.

His seventh video was posted this morning. It began in his usual close up. He knew his good looks were good for him. "Hello beautiful souls. I can see the daffodil returning to life has touched many of you. And I also know that there are so many videos out there made with special effects that it's hard to truly believe my powers are authentic."

He carved a light ball from the space in front of him again.

"I can tell you I don't simply create this light ball out of thin air. I am gathering light particles from the fabric of our universe. Yes, the *fabric* of our universe. What is on the other side of this fabric?"

He carved again into the thin air. Clawing even. The effort exhausted him. But for the briefest of moments, he scraped enough light from the air that it appeared to open a tiny hole into another place. Maybe into another plane?

"Did you see that? See that brief window into something other than my reality. It's another world. Those who want to dismiss it, will find their proof. Those who need to believe, will find theirs. But tomorrow is Thanksgiving, and after everyone enjoys time with food and family I am going to livestream my greatest miracle yet. I am going to open a portal to this other world and show you what's on the other side. But I don't want it to be limited by the internet's understandable skepticism. I know I need first hand witnesses for our common faith to grow. So I am asking for viewers who may have an audience of their own. Influencers, reporters, writers. Come share Thanksgiving with me on my family's Indiana farm. Bring your cameras, your computers, your eyes, and your open — or closed — minds. Be first hand witnesses for others. For it is time to show you that I can open doors to new worlds. It is time for the age of spiritual magic to begin."

Shepherd took a deep breath, focused on the light ball in his hands. The camera pulled backwards until we could see his entire body. For thirty seconds nothing happened. But then the light expanded as tall and wide as a doorway, obscuring him behind it. Shepherd stepped through the light and addressed the camera again in a close up. "Step into the light with me, my beautiful souls." The video ended.

I rewinded it to the moment he went through the light. As with walking through the wall, the act itself did not impress me. It was the tiny particles of electric light that still danced on his shoulders, in his hair, on his eye lashes. These details were not something online creators had the time, money, thought, or patience to produce. Even most Hollywood films wouldn't bother spending their fx budget on it.

Did all these small hints of authenticity make me believe this Shepherd truly knew magic?

No. Most likely, he was a smart enough creator to know that these details would help him stand out.

Yet I still desperately *wanted* to believe.

I needed to believe.

In something. Anything. Bigger than myself.

So I sent a direct message:

---

Shepherd:

I'm a writer for the Quest College newspaper and would be honored to attend your Thanksgiving event as a first hand witness. I promise an open mind.

Cyur

---

Eight minutes later, he responded:

---

Dear Cyur,

Thank you so much for your interest and your open mind. The four spots for dinner filled up quickly. But I do happen to know your paper's editor is Madison Pike. If she could attend with you, I will make an effort to add two more chairs to our table. I look forward to meeting you.

Your Shepherd

---

MADISON PIKE, my paper's editor, was also the daughter of Michael Pike, chairman of the Pike Media Empire. Second family to the Murdochs in reach and influence within conservative politics. Shepherd was savvier than I would have predicted. I was uncomfortable with savvy. Maybe because I lacked it so completely.

Madison Pike was also the woman referred to by KC as my 'blonde rich girlfriend'.

Madison was a modern cultural icon as everyone, including Shepherd it appeared, knew. Madison was also intimidatingly intelligent and bemoaned even a second wasted on fools.

Madison, however, was not my girlfriend. She was a senior, my boss, and only assigned articles to this lowly, shy sophomore such as, '*Is the new student union behind schedule?*'

KC called her my girlfriend because she knew — without me ever discussing her with KC or anyone else — that I was in love with Madison Pike. Or at least interested in being in love with her. We had never had a conversation beyond two sentences.

And now I would have to look this sophisticated, mental giant in the eyes and tell her I wanted her to skip whatever worldly plans she had with her family and come to Indiana with me for Thanksgiving.

*Why?* She would ask, already laughing at me,

To see if this guy on the internet might be a god.

# THE LOVE INTEREST

QUEST COLLEGE WAS FOUNDED by Shelly Wray in 2003. Ms. Wray was a nun turned author turned early internet pioneer who sold her new age online retail hub, TrU, to AOL in 1999 for twenty-three million dollars. AOL had no idea what they bought. Some could argue AOL had no idea what they themselves were and TrU was shuddered as AOL descended into irrelevancy.

Ms. Wray used her new found fortune to buy a private lake and the surrounding 88 acres in unincorporated northern Wisconsin, north of the resort town Waterfall. She founded and built Quest College from scratch with the stated mission of *A Spiritual Birthplace for the Next Generation of Spiritual Leaders.* While Ms. Wray went out of her way to make sure all religions and spiritual expressions were represented, many of the major Christian branches were offended nonetheless. The admission process was highly unusual from the beginning: you submitted the first fifty pages of a fiction or non-fiction book of your spiritual journey thus far. Equally unusual was that if you were accepted, tuition was free but you agreed to (1) finish the book as a requisite of graduation (2) give 50% of the book's proceeds back to the school.

Quest College remained an obscure if bemusing oddity in higher education until the 2018 publication of Quest graduate Tunisia Washington's book, *We Are Fantasy Creatures All*. The novel's premise was that a Tolkien-esque dimension existed side by side with ours that held our soul's energetic twin. It went from cult favorite to New York Times bestseller within five months. Quest College enjoyed a boon in interest, including my own.

WHEN KC BROKE up with me it also kneecapped my plan to follow her to the University of Georgia, sending my life into a three pronged existential crisis: heart, mind, and soul. I grasped at any book or voice that promised even the faintest answers to my despair, which eventually led me to Washington's book which then led me to Wray's Quest College.

Having never written anything longer than a five

page history report, I puked out the required fifty pages into a rambling, incoherent mess about an insecure teenager who only grows more insecure after he discovers he has supernatural powers. For reasons I still do not understand, Quest College made me one of their 88 freshmen last fall.

With less than five hundred people on campus, including professors and administrative staff, Quest College is smaller than most high schools. Surrounded by a sea of uninhabited woods, the campus center is on Lunar Lake, with just over a kilometer of shoreline. Spread out along the circumference is student housing, classroom buildings, the library, mediation huts, religious temples, and more. Those who started at other liberal arts schools before transferring here insist that this isn't simply moving to a different college campus, it's landing on a different planet.

AFTER THE MESSAGE FROM SHEPHERD, I texted Madison Pike if I could pitch her a story idea to work on over Thanksgiving break. She responded with:

Shoot your shot sophomore

My shot:

> Can I pitch it in person?

She didn't immediately respond. Though I had never verbalized my romantic interest in Madison, she was far too insightful not to know. And her lack of response left me mortified that she was avoiding my story pitch to avoid confronting my romantic one. But eight minutes later:

> A car is taking me to the airport in 25 minutes so you better already be swimming my way.

With no time to consider how her departure made my improbable mission impossible, I showered in two minutes, threw on a gray hoodie, blue jeans, brown boots, and my well-worn navy peacoat.

Students *did* swim to class in early September and late May, kayaked across the lake whenever not frozen, but it was November and I preferred the classic sprint along the shoreline walkway from the sophomore quad to the senior one on the opposite side.

Mid-run, my phone rang. I answered without looking, "Madison, I'm —"

"Madison?  MADISON?!  MADDDISSS-SOOOOON!?" It was not Madison.

"KC, I can't talk —"

"You were supposed to call me!"

"Why —" Oh. Right. "I wasn't going to call you. I haven't called you in a year."

"But when I found you your super-powered Jesus figure, you *were* gonna call me."

"They're just videos..."

"You and I both know there's something more to this guy."

"I have to go."

"You going to his Thanksgiving thing?"

"Bye, KC."

"Cyur!"

I hung up, finished the five hundred meters to Madison's bungalow. As I caught my breath, I blocked KC's number. Cutting off communication with her should be unquestionably beneficial to my mental health. Only the singular, strange, secret bond we shared left the smallest slivers of doubt that I may yet need her in my life.

"Let yourself in, sophomore!" Madison yelled after I knocked. Deep breath. Opened the door.

A KID LIKE ME — average high school student, middle class parents, crippling self doubt that seemingly doubled with every birthday — could only look at the opportunity that Quest College offered as nothing short of a marvel.

But even after the success of *We Are Fantasy Creatures All,* Madison Pike choosing to attend school here made no logical sense, not when the Yales, Stanfords, and Oxfords were there with open doors and bent knees. The publishing power of Quest Press still remained a fraction of the two New York houses her family's empire controlled. Publishers she could probably ask for as a stocking stuffer this Christmas. Even as an act of rebellion in the most inflated psychological analysis of Madison's liberal, feminist war against her father's patriarchal machine didn't add up.

"WHY YOU STANDING THERE? Talk, talk, talk," Madison said as I waited just inside the doorway to the bungalow. She was whirling from her bedroom to the shared living room where her suitcase lay open. Blonde hair, tied high and loose, roots an accidental accent. Black suit, egg shell blouse, black high heeled boots. Madison was American royalty whose disdain for the pretentious only made her all the more regal. She was but two years older than me, yet I felt two decades behind her in maturity.

"I, uh..." Only now did I notice one of her roommates, balled up on the couch under a blanket. Large book in hand, larger headphones over ears.

"Sophomore, come on, this isn't a ruse to ask me out, is it?"

"Um, no..." Not consciously.

"Every year someone on staff thinks that's a good idea, and it inevitably happens around Thanksgiving, and my response is always the same, 'When I want something, that something knows it. And if you have to ask, you don't know, and if you don't know, you're *not* that something.'"

"Right, got it, no... I'm not... I'm here..." *because I want you to come to Indiana with me to see if this online personality has superpowers.*

"Spit it out, sophomore!"

"Yes... actually, can you just look at this..." I opened my phone, found the first light ball video. It was the only piece short enough to capture her attention between the room-to-room sprint. Though she did not suffer fools, and she clearly thought me one at this moment, she was still a good leader and gave me the ninety seconds to watch.

"Cool? Yeah. Cool. You want to do a story about how people on social media are getting as good as Hollywood at special effects? What's this have to do with the core mission of our college and paper? I want answers to the great questions of the universe! Not how some dude who lives with his mom mastered photoshop." She disappeared into the bathroom, dumping toiletries into her large beige purse.

"No. I... think there's a small chance... that this Shepherd is... for real."

"For real what?" Madison yelled out from the bathroom. My eyes fell on the roommate who was looking right at me. *Could she hear me under those earphones?*

I managed, "For real... like created that light ball for real... like he has powers..." As the words left my mouth, the mortification crushed me from every angle. The roommate's eyes popped before she retreated to her bedroom, answering yes, she *could* hear me make a fool of myself.

Madison stopped packing, stepped slowly back out into the living room. After a quick glance at her watch, she marched next to me, grabbed me by the elbow as if I was a misbehaving five year old and placed me on the couch. She sat on the coffee table, looming as the frustrated but loving parent. "Xavier... wait, you have a nickname you like right?"

"Cyur, but you can call me what —"

"Like 'Sire' as in king?"

"No, it sounds the same as Sire but spelled C-Y-U-R."

"Then why — never mind. You want to be Cyur, you're Cyur. Listen. I get it. No one, not even me, comes to school here without a major, major hole in their chest —" She poked my sternum with her index finger. The touch quivered through me. "— that hole that most people on this planet fill with religion, and if not religion with work or family or art, and if not those with drugs and video games and other addictions like love. Ha. But seriously, I get it. Me, you, and most people on campus came here because we want to know — not want, *need to know* — why the hell we are here and what's it all mean. And here's the crappy part about needing to know something like this above everything else: we've made our life obsession something *no one* can answer with finality. We started a quest — at Quest College, ha — that has no finish line. But even worse than us *knowing* there's no finish line is that almost everyone else — who thinks about these big questions a tiny fraction as much as us — is convinced with absolute confidence that there is one. Because since the moment the first human asked '*why are we here?*' there were fifty conmen crackpots selling Heaven or righteousness or whatever booby prize at the end of life's rainbow got them money and power." She looked at her watch.

"I should let you finish getting ready to go —" It was for the best.

Madison looked up, smiled, caught her breath, then said, "Yes, but no. Yes, but let me finish. I get it. I'm sure you think me and you are from different worlds.

And actually, maybe we are. But we're on the same mission. And on this mission there are only a few of us. The searchers. Searching for meaning above all else — more than money, more than love, more than power. Meaning. *Meaning*. And because we want it so, so, *so* bad sometimes we get tired and when we tire, we latch onto the closest life raft. I'm mixing metaphors, but you're following. We latch onto that close life raft and only when we have rested up a bit do we realize that life raft wasn't a life raft it was just a mirage put there by one of those crackpots we loathe so much and we have to keep swimming. Because, Cyur, that's what this so much older than you twenty-one year-old woman thinks might be the only provable meaning to any of this."

She stopped. It all sounded very wise. I was more confused than ever.

"None of what I said made any sense, did it?"

"It did."

"No, it didn't. Just because I'm your boss and you have a crush on me doesn't mean you can't tell me I don't know anything. That's what us searchers all have in common! We know none of this makes sense! And that drives us insane!" Her eyes fell to her watch again. "I really have to go." She leapt up, zipped her suitcase, ran back to the bathroom for her purse. Her phone rang. She winked at me, which stopped my heart, as she said, "Want to earn some brownie points and carry my bag out to the car?"

"Of course," I said and did as told.

Madison answered her call as she raced ahead outside, "Dad, the car just got here. I'll be in New York by five. Where's dinner?" She listened as I followed. Something changed. A cloud fell over her face, revealing, however briefly, someone less assured and worldly than the Madison I had always known. Her pace slowed to a stop. She spun to look back toward the lake, allowing me to witness eyes glisten with contained heartbreak. "Well, Dad, actually, that is *not* okay. No. None of it. Yeah, it actually sucks. Like *you* suck. Um, no, I'm not gonna grow up. I'm gonna say fuck off and then hang up is what I'm gonna do. So ready? Here it comes: Fuck you, Dad." And she hung up.

Madison took a moment, closed her eyes, breathed deep. Gave her wounded inner child a patient hug, then opened her eyes and smiled at me with returned sophistication.

"Most people think I'm rebelling against my father. Ha. I wish. No, just classic daddy abandonment issues. If I thought for one second me pretending climate change wasn't real and women should be breeding slaves for men would get my dad to love me, I'd do it. I'm kidding. Maybe. The point is it wouldn't do crap. He was never going to have dinner with me tonight.

He was never going to be in town for the holiday. There was always going to be some new business or new girlfriend far more interesting than me."

"I'm sorry," I said. For the first time since I met her, I understood why Madison was here at Quest College. For the first time, I could relate to her instead of just worship her.

"Anyyyyyyyyway, got any plans this week I can crash?"

My face went stiff.

"Sophomore, I'm kidding..."

"Actually..."

# 3

# THE ROAD TRIP, PART ONE

## (CAMPUS TO BATHROOM)

MADISON CONVINCED HERSELF. I just tried to not screw it up.

Once I explained that Shepherd requested her personally, and then showed her the rapidly expanding viral nature of his videos, she rattled off, "Okay, okay, okay, I see it, this is great actually. The next generation of spiritual leaders — especially when this whole Meta-verse thing happens — are gonna be born and thrive through crap like this. And it will be the responsibility of people like us — the searchers, the educated bullshit detectors — to show the world that these are just the future's televangelists. Right?"

I could only nod, because:

"Except you really think this stuff is real?" She tried, hard, not to express scorn. It was impossible. "That's fine. Great even. You'll be the open mind, I'll be the closed one and we'll write the article together. I'll see if I can get it in the Times. God, that would really piss off my dad. So what do we need?"

"It's an eight hour drive. I was planning on driving."

"That's sounds like torture. But great, I feel like being tortured. You have a car? You drive? I'm a no on both."

"Yes and yes."

But when I showed her my blue Civic from the previous century, she said, "On second thought, I prefer my torture in a Range Rover with a professional behind the wheel." She led me back to the driver still waiting by her bungalow. "Hey, sorry, not going to the airport. But can you drive us to Indiana?"

"$100 an hour plus gas," he said, clearly ready for the whims of the rich.

"Done." Back to me, "Go pack a bag, sophomore, we're road tripping like Kerouac. Except, you know, in a fancy SUV with Wifi. Ha."


I THREW UNDERWEAR, socks, and t-shirts alongside my laptop into a backpack. There was a high probability Madison would ditch me in Indiana, if not sooner, but it was worth the risk no matter the odds. When I wrote Shepherd that Madison and I were on our way, he messaged back, "This is a sign from the universe, my new friend," included his phone number, the farm address, and ended with, "If you get to Indiana today, you both are welcome to stay the night here. The other four Thanksgiving guests are all staying here and it would feel wrong not to have Madison here tonight as well."

Interesting, but understandable, he would only mention Madison and not me.


AS WE DROVE OFF CAMPUS, I noticed a black Cadillac sedan waiting across the road from the gate house. Two figures inside. Difficult to see their faces. It followed us as we turned south toward Green Bay. Madison noticed me noticing. "I can see you trying to kick into 'I'm a man, I must protect the princess outside the castle walls', but, sophomore, that looks like standard issue security detail my a-hole dad hired to buy himself a guilt-free week after I cancelled the NetJet flight to New York."

I nodded. What I didn't say was that I had seen that car before. *Dozens of times*. Madison already thought my grasp of reality was tenuous.

"And, also, sophomore, you should know — I ain't the princess in my story. I'm the goddamn warrior hero."

"I know you are," I said, without hesitation, which caught Madison off guard.

"All right then. Maybe you and I are gonna be friends after all." She held out her hand for a fist bump. I met it as if it was oxygen. "Now, let's get to work." She took out her laptop. I did the same. "But first, as they say, coffee." She laughed and directed the driver to the only Starbucks within thirty miles.

WATCHING THE SHEPHERD VIDEOS AGAIN, this time through Madison's now caffeinated eyes, I felt and thought everything I did upon first viewing. Only more so. He was incredibly attractive, but used it to invite the viewer in not to show us up. He always led with his reverence of the magical, the mystical, the spiritual. The view count was beside the point. And though the acts themselves were not impressive or original by popular entertainment standards, the details remained deeply compelling in their almost imperceptible nature.

"I don't get it, what about his ear?" Madison asked after I pointed at it.

"It's bleeding."

"My ear bleeds, too, sophomore. Him walking through the wall is supposed to be the show."

"But if this is just an act —"

"Not if, *it is*, but go on —"

"Most magicians wouldn't think about having an ear bleeding with a wood splinter. Nor would they want their audience thinking about their bleeding ear. They'd want you only thinking about them walking through the wall."

"So maybe he knows no other video magician has details like this but super nerds like you — no offense —"

"None taken."

"Super nerds like you notice it, then you post about it and this nerd detail drives more people to watch it, study it, and it's what convinces everyone that this guy isn't a fake like everyone else. *This* one is real... but really he just seems more real because he conned the nerds into vouching for him with his fake detail inside his bigger fake act."

"Agreed."

"What do you mean 'agreed'?"

"I agree that this is, by far, the most likely reason for the presence of details like the wood splinters, the light residue, and his exertion. He knows a few will notice and those few will be his first disciples to recruit his larger flock."

"So you know he's conning you and you still are letting yourself be conned?"

"I..." Couldn't say too much. "I want to believe. Not that just Shepherd is capable of magic. But everyone is."

"That's the key. People like me don't want to believe anyone's special. I've met so many politicians and movie stars and billionaires and they're all so... *average*. I admire their influence and opportunities, but it's not like I feel they are different than me. In fact, frankly, most are a lot duller in both mind and presence. They just need it more. Need the attention. Like my dad. He just needs to feel relevant. He'd trade every dime he ever made just to feel relevant."

"And you just want to be relevant to him," I said, which hit her like a slap to the cheek. "I shouldn't have said that."

"No, no... it's okay. I like you speaking your mind! Yeah. Maybe. Maybe you're right. Maybe everything I do is just to make myself relevant to him. He's got a thousand women that will tell him he's brilliant and important. He's got a thousand employees that will do everything he says. But for me to be relevant, I have to be something he couldn't have thought could be relevant. So I go to this cult college in nowhere Wisconsin and write about the search for the meaning of life."

"I think it's great," I said.

"Well, that makes one of us because saying it out loud makes me feel like an idiot. A naive, clueless child. Because guess what? I've never felt less relevant to him than at this exact moment." She closed her laptop, tossed it back in her purse. "I'm going to take a nap and try to forget about all my terrible life choices, including going on this ridiculous road trip to Indiana."

I said nothing. Quiet was my default state, but even more so when someone was visibly upset. Just never felt qualified to help and always likely to make it worse.

I STOLE glimpses of Madison asleep against the window. Though nervous I'd screw this up somehow, riding beside her sleeping in the back of a car also felt cosmically destined. Maybe it was because I had a crush on her since the moment I saw her, maybe because her physical and intellectual attributes had been sold to me as desirable by society my entire life. But I preferred to believe it was, as she just mentioned, our common existential quest. For almost everyone else there's a defined finish line. For the fundamentalist it's God and heaven, for the atheist it's the finality of death. For everyone between true believers and true disbelievers, it's some compromise between the two endgames that allows them to sleep at night and not stress about it during the day.

For us, the *searchers* as she calls us, we have thought about it too much to ignore the holes in both fundamentalist and atheist arguments. And once you see the holes, they get bigger. And the bigger they get, the more questions arise to fill those holes. And with more questions, less sleep at night and less peace during the day.

The major difference between Madison and me was not insignificant. The way she spoke of it, she was sure her quest would never have a finish line. That the search itself was the point. Her inner peace would come when she accepted the search was not *for* inner peace but rather the search *was* the inner peace.

I couldn't.

I had to believe there was an end to my search.

I had to believe someone or something was out there bigger and more important than me. Someone that could tell me what all this means and what we are supposed to do with all that meaning. A long time ago that someone was my mom. Then it was Flame. Then it was KC. And today I'm hoping that person is in Indiana.


"YOU A VIRGIN?" Madison asked.

I had stopped stealing glances of her sleeping and instead was gorging on them. So it took me a moment to realize she was awake and catching me in my indulgence.

"Sophomore, only a virgin stares at me the way you're staring at me..."

"Sorry."

"Listen, kid, once you have sex with a girl — any girl really but especially one you think you're in love with — you'll stop thinking women are the answers to your problems."

"I don't... I mean, I'm not..."

"Not a virgin? Quest is a small campus and the paper is microscopic. Sad to say, but I'd have heard."

"I haven't been with anyone since college started because..." *I have been in love with you, Madison...* "But I had a girlfriend in high school ."

"And was she as... you know... as you?"

"Nerdy and shy?"

"Your words, but yes, those work."

I laughed. "No, KC is a... she's a force of nature."

"Picture."

"Huh?"

"I want to see a picture of her. Now I'm curious."

"I don't have any."

"You don't have any pictures of your first love on your phone? What about your socials?"

"I'm not on social media."

"Is this one of those 'I had a girlfriend in Canada' things?"

I didn't have any photographs because I was trying to extract her from my life, not keep her there. But the infinitely small chance of convincing Madison I was not entirely pathetic required me to let KC back in my life in this small way. "You can google her. Kahina Charlette Jackson."

Madison's fingers shot to her phone. I looked out the window. "Ha!" She said, then, "Come on, kid. You're making this weird. This is a game an 8th grader would play. Pretending you dated a girl like this to impress me. You realize the ex-president's son still sends me dick pics, right?"

I let my head drift from the safety of passing scenery toward Madison's enflamed gaze. But I could not brave words against her building fire.

She did not hold back: "Oh, boy, you got a stalker vibe going now. Seen it a million times. This was a mistake getting in a car all day with you. Sophomore, listen. Even if I wasn't your boss, even if you weren't two years younger, even if you weren't unbearably shy, I am attracted to men who know exactly who they are and you have *not one fucking clue* who you are supposed to be. You dress half preppy, half grunge, all dork. Hair caught between long and short, a beard you can't grow out but try anyway, and big, lost Bambi eyes begging for a shotgun between them to put you out of your misery. You're insecure, you're awkward, you live in some fantasyland in your head. I mean, look at this woman —" She held a photograph of KC after she scored at an U-21 USWNT match in Spain this summer. "She's on the national soccer team! And she's fucking gorgeous. *And* she must have you by three inches and can out bench you by fifty pounds! It would be like Serena Williams dating the skinny white boy who fetches tennis balls for her!"

I nodded my head. *What could be said?*

"You always nodding your head is really creepy."

I nodded again.

"Stop nodding!"

Steeling myself, I managed, "I am interested in you, Madison. Deeply. And I have not pursued anyone else at college because I cannot settle for someone less when someone like you remains close, however intangible. But I would not misrepresent myself for any gain. Even for the gain of you."

Madison leaned toward the driver, but not before shooting back at me, "Never mind. Nodding is actually less creepy than you talking like you're in some 19th century romance novel." Then ahead to the front seat, "Driver — Mark, right? — Mark, how soon until we reach Milwaukee?"

"Seventy minutes, ma'am."

"Too long. I need to use the bathroom. So stop at the cleanest gas station you can find. And then you're going to drop me at the Milwaukee airpot before you take the boy here to Indiana." When she leaned back into her seat, face already buried on a travel app, she said, "While I'm sure your imaginary girlfriend KC Jackson, in addition to being a world class athlete and part time super model, was also nice and patient and saved abandoned puppies, it's good you see me for what I am: a fickle, spoiled bitch. Once you see that I'm not here to save you, maybe you'll grow up and save yourself."

2:29 PM

COFFEE DIARRHEA. ALWAYS FUN. PROBABLY WAS AN ASS TO THE SOPHOMORE CUZ I WAS ABOUT TO SHIT MY PANTS. I'LL APOLOGIZE BEFORE I DITCH HIM AT THE AIRPORT. I JUST CAN'T TAKE ANOTHER SECOND OF SERVING HIS GF SAVIOR COMPLEX. OVER IT. ONLY HIRING FEMALE STAFFERS NEXT SEMESTER

2:37 PM

THIS SHEPHERD VIDEO GUY JUST TEXTED ME. SAYS HE KNOWS I'M HAVING SECOND THOUGHTS BUT IT'S IMPORTANT TO THE UNIVERSE WE MEET. DON'T KNOW WHAT'S WORSE: THE SOPHOMORE BEING SCARED OF HIS

OWN SHADOW OR NARCISSISTS LIKE THIS GUY WHO THINK HE'S THE SUN THAT CASTS THE SHADOWS. TEXTED SHEPHERD BACK THAT CYUR SHOULDN'T HAVE GIVEN HIM MY NUMBER, THEY'RE BOTH STALKERS, AND I'M GONNA BLOCK HIM.

2:43 PM

STILL ON THE TOILET. NEVER DRINKING COFFEE AGAIN.

2:47 PM

SHEPHERD TEXTS ME AGAIN BECAUSE I'M TOO BUSY POOPING TO BLOCK HIM:

SHEPHERD

I've thought about what I could share that would inspire you to come for more profound reasons than my returning a flower to life.

The answer is nada

SHEPHERD

Humbly then, I'm sending you my latest video — made primarily for you — in the hope that there is still an opportunity to meet you.

2:54 PM

DIARRHEA HAS DONE ITS THING, BUT I CAN'T MOVE FROM THE TOILET. CAN'T TEXT THIS SHEPHERD BACK. THE LINK HE SENT HASN'T MADE ME THINK BETTER OF HIM. IN FACT, IT'S PISSING ME OFF. **MORE EVERY SECOND**. NOW I WANT TO BURY THIS GUY. EXPOSE SHEPHERD FOR THE SMALL, SMALL, PATHETIC FRAUD HE IS.

# 4

# THE ROAD TRIP, PART TWO

## (BATHROOM TO FARM)

MADISON LEFT the gas station bathroom, eyes in search of me. When I turned to face her, her body wiggled, as if freeing itself from an uncomfortable thought.

"Let's go, sophomore," she yelled, "I pooped the bitch in me out and this ludicrous adventure to Indiana is back on."

Only after we were back on the highway did I notice Shepherd had posted another video. A close up. Eyes big. A sparkle in them. Almost as if added for effect. He spoke slowly, emotions held barely in check. "Many have asked what world I will open a portal to tomorrow. Well, as you know, I have posted videos of bringing flowers back to life. What you don't know is that I do this by finding the flower's spirit in the next life. So this portal to another world is not just a portal to any world... it is a portal to our next world. The afterlife. For many reasons, I was hesitant to tell you. But now my most anticipated witness is having second thoughts about attending. So I feel compelled to share that tomorrow, shortly after two p.m. eastern time, I will open a door to the land of the dead and bring back to life... a person. Not just anyone. But someone special to this witness. Despite her skepticism of me never being higher, tomorrow she will see what cannot be denied. Tomorrow she will become a believer. I hope you will, too."

I snapped my head toward Madison, who said, "He's talking about me..."

"And your mom."

"Listen, sophomore, I'm fine. She's been dead over ten years. I'm over getting sad about it. But a con artist like this using her for his con? I'm angry. I'm raging. And now I need to burn this guy to the ground."

"I'm sorry."

"Don't be sorry. Be as angry as I am that this guy thinks he can get away with it."

. . .

DUE TO MADISON'S father's fame within media, her mother Lily's death was national news. Suicide. Slit wrists, then jumped from her bedroom balcony into the pool. Madison found her. She was eight years old. Her father tried to hide the cause, but he couldn't buy the silence of the most crucial witness: his daughter. Michael Pike's political ambitions died with his wife.

MADISON SPENT most of the next hour alternating from writing in her phone to writing in her laptop. I tried to do the same but was too consumed with what Shepherd was attempting and why. If his powers were real, why focus so much of it on Madison? And if he was a fraud, why risk so much on Madison's reaction to his trick?

"YOU NOTICE ALL THESE BILLBOARDS?" Madison said, pointing outside, snapping me back to the present.

"I had not."

"For the past hour, every billboard was of two ilks. Telling women every life is precious and abortion is against God's will. Or the billboard was an advertisement for an adult shop where a man could hunt his favorite masturbation material. Wisconsin's one of the most 50/50 states in the country and I'm sure some would think this is an example of that. But do people not see this is really both hands of the patriarchy? Right hand: Men, you deserve to orgasm with abandon, let us assist with all of your desires! Left hand, Women, you are but vessels for the male's orgasm, do not dare waste it with your own desires!"

I nodded. Then tried —

"Oh, stop trying *not* to nod now! That's even creepier than your nods."

"Sorry."

"And don't say sorry! We got — Mark, how much longer to the farm?"

"GPS says just over five hours, ma'am."

"We got five hours left. I need you as my partner, not some smitten yes boy. Okay?"

"Okay."

"Not convincing in the slightest but we're stuck with each other so let's roll. Find out this Shepherd's real name, and if you find that, find out where he works, if he went to college, all that. I have a couple other people looking but no one has found out anything yet and maybe you'll have better luck."

"Will do."

"Also, Cyur, I know this big miracle of his is tomorrow..."

"After the Thanksgiving dinner. He's going to live stream it."

"Did he mention anything about meeting him tonight?"

"He did say we could stay at his farm. I assumed you would prefer a hotel."

"Yeah, yeah, for sure... no way I'm sleeping on hay in a barn or whatever he has in mind... but maybe tell him we're gonna be in town early and would love to meet him tonight if possible."

"Will do."


I WAS glad to have a specific task assigned to me. If I had been approaching this as a journalist from the moment I saw his first video — and not as a lost soul in search of a miracle — I would have already done this research. Which might have impressed Madison. Or, at the very least, kept her from looking upon me with nothing but dismissive pity.

Using the number he messaged earlier, I texted:

> Madison and I will stay at a hotel but would love a chance to meet you tonight if possible.

SHEPHERD

Still hope you stay the night. But, yes, please come by the farm tonight. The rest of tomorrow's guests will already be here.

Both of us would also like some background on you.

SHEPHERD

Madison asked for this?

We both need it.

SHEPHERD

You're in the car with her now.

I didn't answer.

SHEPHERD

Short bio attached.

I deleted old socials once my calling called;)

When and how did your calling call?

He did not text back immediately. To formulate?

SHEPHERD

Can I leave some answers as a reward for coming tonight?

Yes. Understood.

SHEPHERD

Can I ask you a question?

Yes, you may.

SHEPHERD

Are you and Madison in a relationship?

No, she is my editor.

SHEPHERD

But you wish for more.

I detested lying, but I also detested this question.

She is my editor.

SHEPHERD

Well answered. Excited to meet you both.

I FORWARDED Shepherd's biography over to Madison.

"How'd you find this?" she asked the moment it landed on her phone.

"I asked him for it."

"Ha. Nice. Sometimes your earnest straight forwardness has its advantages."

<u>SHEPHERD COTTAGE</u>
BORN TWENTY-SEVEN YEARS AGO,
WEST WOODS, INDIANA
ATTENDED PUBLIC SCHOOLS,
DIDN'T MAKE THE FOOTBALL TEAM
COMMUNITY COLLEGE FOR ONE SEMESTER
VARIOUS WORK, INCL. BARISTA AND UBER DRIVER
ARRESTED FOR PUBLIC INTOXICATION, CHICAGO
DISCOVERED MAGIC
CHANGED THE WORLD, THIS THANKSGIVING

"WITH THIS RESUME, giving himself that name, I think he's still crafting his hero origin story."

"Sounds like you're starting to think he's a fraud," Madison said, then focused on my face for my response.

"No more now than before. In fact, if his powers were real... and they only recently manifested, then he's still trying to figure out who he is and who he's supposed to be."

Madison bounced her head in brief thought, "I don't know... if I had superpowers, I'm pretty sure I'd never be unsure of anything again. Especially myself."

I resisted my instinctual nod. For several reasons I

couldn't ponder now. Instead I said, "Shepherd did say we could go there tonight."

"Great," Madison said, only for her left shoulder to twist involuntarily.

"You okay?"

"No, but also yes," she said, then returned to her writing.


THE TWO HOURS it took to pass through Milwaukee and Chicago were spent further digging what I could on Shepherd. The farm address where we were going was owned by a Sebastian Cottage, which could be a relative. Though a search for Sebastian Cottage produced no relevant results. The item that interested me most from his bio was the 'arrested for public intoxication'. Everything else had a romantic generality to it. Public intoxication was neither. It allowed me to scan through police blotters and arrest records from the last two years. There was no Shepherd Cottage. I googled the forty-two names of every male between 20 and 35. None were Shepherd. But one — a blonde guy in a fraternity sweater — had the same sea green eyes. As if they could be distant cousins. His name was Henry Simanski.

Night had fallen by the time we stopped for gas, restrooms, and snacks just past Gary, Indiana. Madison, with her large bag of Flamin' Hot Cheetos and Diet Coke, eyed my water and bag of almonds with suspicion.

"Didn't take you for a health nut, sophomore."

"Not by choice. I love junk food. And pizza. And burgers. And French fries. And milk shakes most of all... but I get unpleasantly ill. Unless I'm by myself with a toilet nearby, the risk-reward is unfavorable."

She laughed. "See? That's great. Be real. Trust me, when you meet the right girl, being honest about yourself will be the fastest way to her heart."

ONCE BACK ON THE HIGHWAY, Mark let us know we would be there in 90 minutes.

Madison's breath quickened. Her legs alternated jitters. I couldn't read her face. But she could read me attempting to.

"Listen, Cyur... I..." She tried to laugh again. It wasn't convincing. "I'm fine. Yeah, fine. Okay?"

"Okay."

"Again, you're a terrible liar. But, in this case, I approve." She closed her eyes and took a deep breath. "Don't suppose you have any low key edibles, do you?"

I shook my head. "I don't..."

"It's fine. You're probably the only one at school that wouldn't have any, which is just great to have you as a travel partner. I'm kidding. Seriously. Not your problem."

"I'm sorry."

"He texted me…"

"Shepherd? How'd he get your number?"

"I assumed you…"

"I would never without your permission."

"I strangely believe you. But that's not the weird thing…"

When she couldn't continue her thought, I said, "I should have told you he had shown signs of being interested in you on a personal level."

She laughed. Which was better than panic. "You think I'm having anxiety because this dude wants to sleep with me?"

I don't know.

"Listen, sophomore, he — like you — probably does have a female savior complex."

"His interest in you would be very different than mine."

"No and yes…" She started, then between her attempted deep breaths, "Someone like you, who has never fit in anywhere, is sure you will be rejected by the whole world. So you become convinced if just one special woman loved you, it would protect you from the world's lack of love. Someone like Shepherd waltzes through life convinced the whole world worships him... except deep down he's afraid he's a fraud. So he thinks if he can convince one woman to love him then that will prove *to himself* he's not a fraud."

"Okay."

"You and your okays and your nods!"

"Sorry."

"And your sorrys!" Yelling was easier for her than breathing.

"Madison, you're right. You're very insightful. I didn't mean to cause more stress."

She closed her eyes, placed her hands over her chest, and labored methodically through her breaths. I hoped she would get a bit more rest before we met Shepherd. Tonight, even if the possible outcomes were wildly divergent, was bound to be eventful.

"MADISON," I said, as we exited the highway into West Woods. She stirred awake.

"Shit..." she mumbled, then jolted upright. "Oh, my, god. We're here?"

"Ten minutes, ma'am," Mark said from the front.

"Do you want to go directly there?" I asked. "Should we find a hotel first?"

She grew still, gazing ahead as if through time. "Fuck it. Let's just get this over with. Right? Yes, let's."

"Okay."

"Your *okays* need their own subtitles."

Madison held up well until we turned off the local road onto an unpaved drive. Her chest was now heaving.

I said, "Mark, let's stop here for a moment." I turned to her. "Madison, we don't have to go. Our mental health is more important than any of this."

"Ha!" She laughed. "Come on, sophomore. Don't attempt to be the white knight. Not your lot in life. So, yeah, now you're seeing that I'm only half fickle bitch... the other half is anxiety crippled child. The bitch is usually the Captain on display for you and the staff at the paper, at class, at parties, back in New York. But when this child wants to take over, I'm helpless."

"We could wait until tomorrow's event," I said.

Madison tried to subdue her breaths but it was only making it worse. "You want to solve my stress?"

"If I can."

"This Shepherd — this conman — needed you to see this video, and for you to show me, and for me to agree to come. He doesn't seem like the type to say 'abracadabra', here's Maddie's dead mom, and then bring out some look-a-like. What's his angle? How's he think he's gonna trick me?"

"If he's a fraud..."

"I can't with your 'if'. Can't. He's a fraud just like

every other wannabe messiah, including ol' Jesus C. himself, was a fraud. But I know you study the frauds even as you hope they're not one. So what's his plan."

"A look-a-like, as you said, would be briefly compelling followed by irrefutable proof it was fake when this woman was interviewed and fingerprinted. So Shepherd will probably have us inside a room he can control then use hidden projectors to create this portal. Or maybe the portal is a practical effect he has already built and then he uses projectors to cast your mom's moving image onto the portal. The image will disappear as you or others run toward it. He will collapse, exhausted from the effort. He will apologize for not being able to keep her alive longer. You'd be angrier than ever but for those brief seconds when you saw her projected image, the video footage of your reaction will be unconsciously compelling to everyone watching online."

"That's really smart analysis, sophomore. Now I'm prepared for his con."

"I must allow there's still a small chance his powers are real."

"And now I think you're a naive sucker again. The world is back to normal."

"I'm glad you feel better."

"At your expense!"

"I don't mind."

"Ha. Oh, Cyur... this dutiful puppy love operating program in your brain is not, in the slightest, alluring on a romantic level. But... it did just talk me back from the panic attack mountain I was about to plunge off of. So thank you for that."

"No problem."

"Now I'm fired up. Let's go roast this asshole."

I nodded.

BUT AS WE rolled ahead down the dirt road toward the farm, I let one thought linger: if Shepherd was not a fraud, Madison's panic attack at seeing her dead mother would dwarf the one I just witnessed. And that made me worry not just for Madison but also for how I would, or could, respond.

.

# THE WIZARD AND THE COURT

"WHAT KIND OF FARM IS THIS?" Madison asked, pointing at the pine trees suffocating the road at every turn. As if we were entering a thick Wisconsin forest rather than an Indiana farm.

"Though overgrown and neglected, you can still sense they were planted in neatly laid rows. My guess is this was a Christmas tree farm at one time. Maybe decades ago."

"Smart guess, kid. But tough to make money on Christmas trees when they are all too tall now to fit anywhere except Rockefeller plaza."

EIGHT MINUTES after turning on the dirt road, we got our first sign of light and life. At the bottom of the final hill, nestled in a small clearing was a white Victorian farm house, complete with a wrap around porch, a central rotunda, and three peaked roof lines on the third floor.

A young woman was waiting at the end of a circular driveway, waving at us as we pulled to a stop. Before the woman opened the door, Madison shot to Mark, "Fifty an hour to wait until we're done."

"I like the hundred dollar rate," he said.

"You would. Fine. Just insist on parking right here in case this old farmhouse turns out to be haunted and we need to make a run for it."

"Yes, ma'am."

The Range Rover's back door popped open, the waiting woman said, with an exhausted smile, "You must be Madison and Cyur. I'm Apple..." She paused, then, "Shepherd's assistant." A second pause. "Welcome to his family farm."

Madison stepped out, shaking Apple's hand. "Happy to be here, Apple." Madison took her in. A dark green suit, stretched against her curves. Blouse cut low. Gold hoop earrings, a pretty face overwhelmed by make-up. Her aura matched her smile: too tired to pretend otherwise.

"Shepherd did want me to again invite you to... stay the night here."

"We're gonna find a hotel, but thank you," Madison said.

"Great," Apple said, unable to hide her relief, "Then follow me. Shepherd is excited to meet you both."

As she went up the porch stairs, Madison turned back to me and mouthed, "She's sleeping with him or wishes she was."

I did not react as I had no idea whether this was true or why it mattered.

A GRAND CENTER interior stair met us inside, wrapping two floors skyward. We travelled past it, down a narrow hall that opened into a ski-lodge worthy great room. Unlike the neglected farm, the house was pristine. Soft whites and light browns, furniture and decorations aglow as if staged this morning by an HGTV crew. A dark gray stone fireplace that stretched five meters high and three meters wide provided a fitting focal point at the far side of the room. Windows just as high on either side.

Five people faced the picturesque fire, spread out on the two large, white linen couches.

"Shepherd," Apple said as we crossed the room toward the group. The others all turned toward us, including the man we had come to see. At sight of Madison, Shepherd leapt to his feet. He was even more handsome in person. As if a Disney animator had brought a prince to life. His height, frame, and stride projected strength without intimidation. His eyes grew wide and bright as he approached Madison. Though a step behind her, I could sense Madison's guard drop at the sight of our host. She took his hand the moment it was offered, smiling without reservation. There was an immediate, crackling chemistry that danced between their eyes.

I stood between them. Apple across from me. She sank at the sight of Madison's and Shepherd's connection. Apple *was* in love with him. Didn't matter whether she was sleeping with him or not. The love was not returned. Just as my interest in Madison had never been returned. Unrequited feelings are always easy to spy in others when you've felt it yourself for so long. Whether or not Shepherd had actual magical powers remained to be seen. But seeing how Madison still had not bothered breaking from the handshake, he undoubtedly held a power of some fashion over her now.

I reminded myself that just as I could not make Madison have feelings for me, I could not stop her from having feelings for someone else. Also reminded myself that doing what was right did not always feel good.

. . .

"SO HAPPY YOU TWO ARE HERE," Shepherd said, breaking from Madison's hand to shake mine. "We were just having a light conversation about the meaning of life." He laughed. The kind of laugh that made you want to laugh with him soon.

"No topic could interest Cyur or I more," Madison said.

"Can we get either of you something to drink?"

"Yes, lots of them," Madison said. Shepherd laughed with her. "What is everyone else drinking?"

"The rest of us are being rather boring, drinking sparkling water with lemon and cucumber. But Apple would be happy to get you some wine or perhaps there's something stronger buried in a closet?"

"I'd love the water," I said. Madison shot disapproval.

"Cyur doesn't know he's supposed to offer me cover for my alcohol needs. So I'll take your fancy sparkling water and just resent all of you as I drink it." Everyone politely chuckled.

"Well, thank you, Madison, for the opening to introduce everyone." He placed his hand behind Madison's back and led us the final three meters to the other guests. All four smiled as we approached, but remained in place where they stood from the couch. "At the far end, closest to the fire, is Jamelle Booker." A tall, thin black man with thick glasses nodded a hello. His hair was cut close, he wore a white turtle neck and white pants. Shepherd added, "His pieces on our collective spiritual crisis have appeared in the Times. His book, *The Next Messiah*, was a best seller. I was obsessed with him even before my magic developed so he was one of my first targets and I could not be more flattered that he's here."

I had read Booker's book. He theorized that much of our political and culture divides were actually a societal cry for a new spiritual leader that could bring both sides to a healthy center. If a new leader didn't emerge, he wrote, then false prophets would rise on both sides and the cultural war could become a spiritual then bloody one.

"Sitting in the center here is Katarina Serrano, who has more followers across her socials than all of us combined. She's considered the premiere influencer amongst young intellectuals." Everyone at Quest College knew Katarina Serrano, largely because most students wished they could be her. She had carved out an impressive following on YouTube interviewing a cross-section of young spiritual leaders, but also figures in politics, tech, entertainment, environmental, crypto, and more. The hook to her appeal was that she started every interview as if she was a young fan-girl (she could be no older than 29), but increasingly revealed the depth of her knowledge and the ambition of her questions as the interview went on. She had exposed more than one charlatan.

It did not hurt Katarina that she looked like a young Jennifer Lopez, earning her a legion of nerdy followers who obsessed over her designer clothes and accidental cleavage reveals.

Shepherd pointed to the man at the far end of the couch to my right. "Our elder statesmen here tonight is William Weigel — and still only barely in his forties —"

"Barely *still* in my forties he meant," William said. Polite laughter yet again. This was a generous group. Weigel wore black pants, a red tie, white shirt, and blue sports jacket. He had deep set eyes, a skeletal face that suggested health struggles.

Shepherd continued, "William started a blog back in the early days of the internet in which he theorized that all of existence was a simulation and that it was only a matter of time until someone learned to manipulate reality as if re-writing code. Almost thirty years later, he still maintains his blog and a small but vital following."

"If you think that sounds like the Matrix," William said, "then you're right. I did start my blog years before the movie premiered. For a hot minute, I assumed they stole from me but then realized my idea wasn't that revolutionary but rather a logical thought progression to the internet's emergence. The Wachowskis were just better at marketing." Polite laughter again. I had never heard of William Weigel. His age, his blogger status, and the central theme to his work didn't match the others.

"And on the near edge of this couch is Nikki Kang. She's a reporter for the Post with a passion for leaders and influencers that rose to fame on the internet."

"Let me interject," Nikki said, dressed in jeans, sneakers, and hoodie. Hair in a bun, glasses propped on her head, pen behind one ear, notebook in one hand. "I'm officially a barely paid intern at the Post, never had a solo byline, and mostly here because I was home for the holiday — I grew up outside Indy — and needed an excuse to not be at *home* home. I do have an interest in internet celebrity, which is just celebrity now, right? And who isn't interested in knowing people everyone knows? I follow both Jamelle and Katarina and when they both re-tweeted Shepherd's daffodil video I got interested. I am the least famous person here by far and yet I'm the one talking the most. Shutting up now and for much of the next 24 hours."

"You're wrong about one thing, Nikki," Shepherd said, patting my left shoulder, "Xavier Good here is definitely less famous than you." Again, polite laughter. But uneasy. Probably because this joke came at my expense. An odd choice to make considering how generous Shepherd was being with everyone else.

Madison undercut his joke with, "The kid prefers the name Cyur and I think we should all be called by whatever makes us happy, right, *Shepherd?*"

I thanked Madison with a small smile but she never looked my direction.

Shepherd, frozen briefly by Madison's defense of me, stumbled for a moment, "Yes, well, yes... Cyur. Beautiful name. Anyway, he's a sophomore at Quest College, writes for the school paper under his editor, Madison Pike, who, astonishingly, I now stand beside." Shepherd beamed as he nodded toward her. As if a proud boyfriend. "And Madison has almost no social media presence and yet is far more famous than all of us."

"Yes," Madison said, "if you really want to know how meaningless fame is, in your next life you all should be born the child of a media billionaire." A healthy laugh from all to wash away the one about me.

WHEN I MESSAGED Shepherd a little over eight hours ago, I assumed he was a minor internet personality whose magic shows were most likely staged. But I asked to come to his event because I needed something to believe in and, just as importantly, needed something to do besides spend Thanksgiving by myself. But his wherewithal to get me to bring Madison took me by surprise. That he also had both the ability and gall to invite and lure guests such as a best selling author, a universally respected young influencer, and a Washington Post reporter was downright shocking.

SOMETHING else besides fame and influence connected all the guests beside me. But I could not, or cannot, verbalize it. I assumed I never would.

THE INSTANT SPELL he seemingly cast over Madison suggested Shepherd might not even need his magic to prove authentic to achieve his ambitions. His storybook good looks, easy charm, and obvious interpersonal talents could lead him to places and people I could barely imagine.

Maybe he knew this. Maybe he knew he needed to win over the minds and hearts of people like Jamelle Booker and Madison Pike and Katarina Serrano before his staged videos were upstaged by someone with better special effects. But he used his uniquely labored magic acts to make people — like those here tonight — look twice. Then his physical beauty and warm words to convince us to stick around for a bit longer. And then, once we met him, and are charmed by his being charmed by us, when we recognize how effortlessly he can stand in the company of authors and billionaire heirs, we decide we might not even care if his magic is an act.

In fact, if Shepherd really can wield true supernatural powers — along with all his human ones — then there is no guessing what he might be capable of.

Changing the world?

Leading the world?

Destroying the world?

None of it could be dismissed.

# 6

# THE CONVERSATION

"SO WAS THERE A CONSENSUS ANSWER?" Madison asked after gulping down half the sparkling water Apple handed us.

Confused looks. Except Shepherd. "She means the meaning to life. No consensus. But all worth noting. Shall we recap ours for her?"

Jamelle spoke first, "We must answer when the universe calls."

"Love that answer," Shepherd said.

"Maximize the good you put back into the world, minimize the bad," Katarina said.

"Also perfect," Shepherd added.

William said, "I was raised by a very Jewish father and a very Catholic mother. Add those together and you get 'Don't piss off God'."

Madison asked, "They didn't make you choose?"

"Oh, my mother definitely chose for me. But in forcing me to her side, I naturally leaned back to his. But the power Catholicism can hold over young kids is rather effective and its bigger threats and bribes are hard to ignore. Thus my summation of 'Don't piss off God... and you'll be okay.'"

Madison noted, "Well, good, I'm glad we have someone representing traditional religion, even if you're a bit clever with it. This would have been a boring conversation if we were all new age liberal assholes." Madison then turned to Nikki. "Miss Post, what's your take on the meaning of life?"

"Don't be an asshole," she said. Everyone laughed, authentically.

"I like it," Madison said, "That might be the one answer I could believe in. Couldn't follow it. But I could believe in it."

Shepherd asked, "And you, Madison, do you have your own answer?"

"Actually we were discussing it this morning. Sophomore, did we come up with anything as clever or profound as theirs?"

All eyes turned to me. I squirmed, but managed, "I believe you said that the meaning of life is the search for the meaning of life."

Jamelle said, "Your answer is both clever and profound."

"Well, Cyur here did a great job editing my rambling nonsense. Obviously he deserves a raise. If we paid our writers." Another laugh from the group. Madison had full control of the room, as she always did at the paper. Not surprised she could do it so quickly and masterfully with a group of older and distinguished people, but I was more impressed than ever by her nonetheless.

"And you, Cyur," Katarina asked, "is your answer the same as Madison's?"

"I'm sure it is," Shepherd said. Another effort to minimize me. Again, odd.

Madison turned sharply to Shepherd, "What about you, internet magic man, what's your answer to the meaning of life?"

Shepherd began, "Well..."

But Katarina stopped him. "I'd love to let Cyur finish his thought before we move on to our host." This interjection by Katarina pissed off both Madison and Shepherd. It also reminded everyone of her unique gifts. All eyes fell back on me. Again, I withered under the attention. But I knew I had to speak and speak authentically:

"I believe all your answers are beautiful, including Madison's... and I can see your answers give each of you a sense of wholeness, and that wholeness gives you confidence to hold yourself in an esteemed group such as this. But none of your answers — nor any I have heard outside of yours — have quelled my doubt or filled that void inside me. So I must keep searching for what makes me whole until I have that same sense you all have today."

Nobody spoke. Shepherd stared at me. If not through me. Madison couldn't look at me at all. William, oddly, took out his phone and texted someone. Katarina finally said, "I had to take a moment to take that in. A very rich answer, Cyur."

"Your answer notwithstanding, if you don't feel equal here, that is our failure not yours," Jamelle said with a smile.

Madison spoke, still not looking at me, "The kid has a way of speaking that's really, *really* alien if it's just the two of you stuck in a car. But in a group like this, I'll admit it has its appeal."

Nikki added, "Let me assure you that I have no such wholeness or confidence. I'm just not as willing to admit it as you." Again, a polite laughter released the tension. Knowing I had distracted from his moment with Madison and the group, I re-directed back to Shepherd:

"Shepherd, thank you for letting me add my small piece. I'm here, maybe more than anyone else, to learn from you. I apologize for the interruption but perhaps it's fitting that you are the final, featured speaker on this topic."

He, unlike Madison, had never looked away from me. I did not know if he was trying to understand my place here or if he was sending me a non-verbal message. A threat even.

Madison finally snapped him from his gaze upon me, "Let's hear it, Sorcerer Shepherd. And it better be as profound as Mr. Booker's, as kind as Ms. Serrano's, as grave as Mr. Weigel's, as funny as Ms. Kang's, as irreverent as mine, and as vulnerable as the sophomore's."

A smile crept slowly over his face, immediately warming the room again. "That's a lot of pressure, Madison," he said.

"I think you like the pressure," Madison said, the flirtation obvious. "What if..." Shepherd started, only to wink at Madison as he snapped his fingers. The overhead lights went dark. The room let out a subdued gasp. Apple was sitting on the far side at the kitchen counter. Her phone in hand. Most likely she was assisting his show through a smart home app. After a moment to allow our eyes to adjust to the now fire-place-lit room, Shepherd continued, "...you are each here representing a voice in all our souls. Jamelle, the grand philosopher. Katarina, the educated progressive. William, the thoughtful conservative. Nikki, the observant skeptic. Madison, the passionate leader. And Cyur, who I thought was here only as the price of Miss Pike's attendance, is our group's spiritual virgin..." The room could not help but snicker. "...if only to help us see where experience has blinded us."

Shepherd's third effort to belittle my presence. Maybe this was his way of including me. Or trying to scare me away. Perhaps sensing my discomfort, he raised his hand toward me, cupping the air between us. A small energy ball formed an arm length in front of my face. The size of a golf ball. White, with tiny black sparks inside it. Another subdued gasp from others. Shepherd then turned to the rest, culling light spheres before them one at a time until there were six dancing in the air, forming a semi-circle. We all reached out to touch the glow. Our hands cut through it, as if not there, though there was a faint warmth inside the light.

Shepherd stood, walked toward the fireplace before turning to face us. "It took me a long time to grasp why I was given the gift of magic, and to what end it should be used. I have determined that I cannot use it only for the benefit of one of those voices each of you represent but I must use my powers to connect all of them. To connect all of us. Not just in this room. But everyone, everywhere." Shepherd twisted his right hand in a gentle circle. The light balls all flew toward him, uniting into a single large light. The size of a basketball. "What if you are each here, not by accident or boredom or my pleading, but because — as Mr. Booker said — the universe called you and you answered."

As he tapped the united light, it disappeared. A second later, the overhead lights came back on. Beads of sweat had formed on his forehead, his chest visibly shook. Out of breath, Shepherd sat on the fireplace hearth, facing us.

"Any questions?"

"Um, yep," Madison asked with smirk. "How the hell did you do what you just did?"

"One of the first things I discovered was my ability to create small light forms. I'm getting quite good at it, though it drains me more than I let on. Until recently, they remained but a harmless light show. Then I discovered the light was really my tearing at the barrier between our world and the next one..."

"Or," Nikki said, "Your assistant Apple is using a smart home app on her phone. And you have tiny projectors hidden in the ceiling and walls." Nikki's skepticism spoke for most.

All eyes turned back to Shepherd, who nodded in agreement, "Yes, that would be more probable than my having supernatural powers."

Madison fired, "Prove Nikki's wrong. Bring Apple

over here, I'll take her phone, and you do the light show again."

"Maybe I could do it again, even though I'm feeling weak now. But does that then threaten my ability to accomplish my much bigger goal tomorrow? Maybe. I want you to believe that I possess true powers so that you can help me use these powers wisely. But I cannot spend my energy — not physical energy, nor mental, nor spiritual — trying to win over every doubter. Even you, Madison. I can only hope the tide of believers slowly wins over all else."

APPLE APPEARED next to him a moment later. As if orchestrated. "Shepherd must now rest. After I help him to his room, I'll come show the rest of you to yours."

Seemingly deteriorating by the minute, Shepherd started gulping oxygen, eyelids drooping. "Sorry for my state. I think I was too excited to show off for you since I hold you all in such high regard. Tomorrow will be different. Tomorrow my powers will finally reach their full strength." Apple put one hand under his right elbow, the other under his right armpit and helped him to his feet. The rest of us watched in silence as they shuffled slowly out of the room and toward the front stairway.

. . .

ONCE SURE THEY were out of earshot, Madison whispered to the rest, "Nikki and I obviously think he's a fraud... the sophomore here wants to drink his kool-aid. Where's everyone else stand?"

Katarina answered first, "His exhaustion appears genuine. He doesn't get defensive like most con-artists do when questioned. At the very least, he seems to believe in his gifts. But I'll hold any more conclusive judgement until I see more than these light tricks."

"Jamelle?" Madison asked.

He let out a long breath, removed his glasses, rubbed his eyes, before putting his glasses back on and speaking: "I still don't understand why I'm here. Maybe because I recently went through a breakup and needed a distraction. Maybe because I'm growing disillusioned even with my own theories. But why choose to spend Thanksgiving at a stranger's instead of at my mom's in Virginia? You cannot comprehend the meal I'm missing tomorrow. He flatters me endlessly, but that doesn't explain my investing time and my own money to travel here. I don't believe he has any Merlin-like magical powers. But he has pulled me here against all logic and that has left me open-minded to a greater cause."

William spoke before needing to be asked, "Have

you considered, Jamelle, that you being here — against all logic as you say — was not entirely of your choice?"

"What do you mean?" Katarina asked.

"That Shepherd influenced your decision..."

"His flattery did not hurt his cause, but —"

I had to speak, "You mean Shepherd used his powers to lure us all here?"

"Yes," William said. "Not you, Cyur. No offense."

"None taken."

"And probably not me or Nikki. But a best selling author, a global influencer, and the heir to the Pike media empire all finding themselves together on an Indiana farm for Thanksgiving... to watch a YouTuber raise someone from the dead? I find it far more likely he used magic to get you here than you all independently found yourselves here for reasons you can't quite explain."

"I'll believe he can raise the dead before I believe he used the force to get me here," Jamelle said.

"I don't know," Katarina started, "I can't explain why I'm here either. Once he messaged me an invite, I couldn't be convinced not to go. My girlfriend thinks I'm again avoiding meeting her parents but I'd actually love to meet her parents. But for some reason I'm here. In Indiana. On a farm." She laughed.

"So then you do think he might have powers?" Nikki asked.

"I'm the flip of Jamelle. I don't believe he can raise the dead. I don't believe he can bring flowers back to life. The light show was, as you said, probably just some fancy electronic trick. But I've met enough charismatic people to believe that the power of persuasion could have supernatural DNA."

Madison turned back to William, "So you're half-Jewish, half-Catholic, believe in traditional religion, but also believe we're all living in a simulation and Shepherd might be our Keanu Reeves? I'm very confused by you, Mr. Weigel."

"I'm confused myself... by myself," he said, and we all smiled. "I know I'm in a room full of over-educated atheists and agnostics, but what your wing of humanity can never explain is: if the universe started not with God but with the big bang, who started the big bang?"

"Physicists now believe cosmic inflation pre-dated the big bang," Katarina said.

"Great," William said, "then who started cosmic inflation?"

"Cosmic inflation and the big bang that followed erased all evidence of what happened before either," Katarina added.

"Which allows anyone who doesn't believe in God to believe that there is a scientific origin story to the universe that the universe just happened to erase as it formed itself."

"And that requires just as much faith as believing in God," Madison said.

"I thought you and I were the skeptics," Nikki said.

"I'm a skeptic of religion... *and of science*. I'm basically a skeptic of anyone who thinks they have all the answers."

Katarina turned back to William, "So you believe God created the universe..."

"Yes."

"And that God created the simulation we all exist in now."

"No."

"Who created that?"

"Probably the devil. Or a bored kid in his dorm room. Or... a charming young man from Indiana."

"Whoah," Madison said, "So Shepherd not only has supernatural powers but he also might be Satan?"

"You're mocking me now. But I'll answer it earnestly. If me — and the Matrix filmmakers and a thousand other people that turned twenty around the birth of the internet — are right about this being all a simulation then it doesn't matter who created it or why. It's a layer — a barrier — between our connection with God. We must tear it down — just like Neo in the Matrix — in order to return man to God's arms."

The room remained silent. William Weigel's zeal

had left a few uneasy. Hard to argue against someone so sure of themselves.

But I found his pattern of thought intriguing and felt he was scratching the surface of some ideas I couldn't yet put words to, so I broke the quiet with: "Though I've never been able to find comfort in a singular God, nor the religions those beliefs formed, I think this idea that reality itself is a barrier to spiritual wholeness is an interesting one."

"It's not reality. It's the simulation that's the barrier," William said.

"But," Jamelle spoke for the first time in a while, "if all we have ever known is the simulation, then the simulation is our reality... and the place we would find ourselves once the simulation was destroyed would seem fantastical to us."

"Yes, I suppose that's true," William relented, annoyed.

"My brain is starting to splinter," Madison said. "To bring it back to my original survey: Nikki and I remain firmly in the 'Shepherd's a fraud' camp. Right?"

"He's a showman. Yes."

"Katarina and Jamelle are in the 'Why the hell am I in Indiana for Thanksgiving?' camp and maybe it's because the universe has its reasons."

"Sure," Jamelle said.

Katarina added, "I just do not believe in coincidences."

"And William is in the 'Shepherd *does* have magical powers... but only because he's an agent of the devil keeping us from being closer with God.'"

"Ms. Pike, if I could be offended this would be that moment."

"Sorry. I'm tired and have had no drugs or alcohol for almost 24 hours and that's making me bitter. Please summarize your view, Mr. Weigel."

William said, "Shepherd's powers are likely real... but only real in this simulation. When we tear down the simulation, all of us will have equal magic in God's eyes."

"Okay. Okay. So what next? We get some sleep and then meet here tomorrow to see if he can bring back my mother from the afterlife?"

Jamelle asked Madison, "No one has asked you how you feel about Shepherd claiming he can and will bring back your deceased mother."

"Including Shepherd," Madison shot with a smirk. Then paused. "How do I feel..." She paused again. "Well, I told the kid it pissed me off and inspired me to come down here and prove Shepherd was a fraud. And since I spend so much of my life thinking there's no point to anything, it was nice to be motivated to do something. I'm also perversely excited about turning the sophomore into a bitter skeptic like me."

Katarina turned to me, "And you, Cyur, still believe his powers are real?"

Madison shot out, "Sorry, right... I keep forgetting none of you were stuck in a car with him for eight hours today. Speak your truth, kid."

To that I said, "I want... need... to believe that there are powers greater than our own. That all of us — including everyone in this room -- are capable of magic. But there's a chance Shepherd's magic, even if real, is not what I came here looking for."

My statement was not succinct enough for anyone to react to with ease, so a silence settled over the room as we all processed what we wanted to witness tomorrow. And what we feared.

Apple returned before another word could be shared by any of us. She said, "Unless anyone needs something to eat or drink, I can show you your rooms now. Madison and Cyur, I've been instructed to again offer you a room to stay in."

Madison asked, "The rest of you are staying here?"
Each nodded.

Madison hesitated for just a moment, "In the small chance this *is* a simulation and this Indiana farm is infected with a software glitch, Cyur and I will find a hotel so at least one or two of us can report what happened. What time should we be back tomorrow?"

"Anytime that suits you. The meal will be served at noon. The event will be live streamed at two."

"Should we bring anything? Besides alcohol. We are definitely bringing alcohol. He doesn't need my mother's scarf or anything to bring her back to life, right?"

"Shepherd asks only for your presence. But you are welcome to bring any drinks you wish."

"Okay. Great. See everyone tomorrow for turkey, stuffing, and my dead mom."

# 7

# THE MOTEL, PART ONE

THERE WAS ONLY one lodging option within twenty miles. A motel, behind a gas station at the base of an abandoned ski hill. Single story, eight rooms. No lights were on save the attendant behind the register. After Mark parked, Madison remained frozen in place, gazing at our singular choice.

She finally muttered, "The Ski Hill Motel... we're going to die here, aren't we?"

"Want me to ask Shepherd if we could stay there after all?"

"Yes. Smart. Much prefer death at his hands than the Norman Bates working here." Off my confusion, Madison added, "You don't know who Norman Bates is, do you? You're better off, trust me."

. . .

I TEXTED SHEPHERD. He didn't answer. Deep asleep if he was half as tired as he last looked. Or pretending he was if it was all part of his show. Fifteen minutes without a response, Madison shot, "Fuck it. Let's be murdered tonight. Mark, you need a room?"

"No, I have another job in Chicago tomorrow morning."

"If Shepherd wasn't so attractive, and if I wasn't utterly dedicated to destroying him, I'd probably ditch this and go back to civilization with you." Madison turned to me. "Get us one room, two beds. If I'm going to die, better you die trying to save me."

"I don't know if that's appropriate..." I said.

"Oh, christ, kid — I'm not going to try to seduce you and you couldn't seduce me if you had ten times the magical powers that Shepherd has. I just won't be able to sleep if I'm jumping at every sound I'm sure is a serial killer breaking into my room."

"Understood. I'll go get the room."

"Here's my credit card —"

"I can pay for this, you've paid for everything else," I said.

"Okay, kid. I'll let you have your moment of chivalry."

. . .

THE STATION ATTENDANT took my sixty dollars, handed me the key to room #8. He never looked up, never said a word. Mark helped us with our bags. Madison fist bumped him good-bye.

The motel room had gray carpet and blue walls. Two twin beds, yellow comforters, white pillows. A small circular dining table by the window, which Madison had me move in front of the door. "Hard to kill us if they can't get in," she said. "I'm gonna shower. Find something on the TV that will make me not think about dying but also not so interesting it keeps me up."

"Okay," I said, standing by the moved table.

"And don't be awkward or I'm gonna think I just trapped myself inside a motel room with the killer."

"Sorry."

"What did I say about saying sorry, sophomore!" She said before closing the bathroom door behind her. After flipping through the two dozen channels offered, I settled on a 1980s Jeff Bridges movie where he plays an unassuming alien.


MADISON EMERGED twenty minutes later in flannel pajama bottoms and a white v-neck t-shirt. No make-up. No bra. I looked away when I realized I was staring.

"All yours," she said. After showering, I put on new

underwear, a new gray t-shirt, and the same jeans. When I then climbed into bed fully clothed, Madison shook her head, "Oh, kid, you are one of a kind."

"How are you feeling?" I asked. She put down the book she was pretending to read, turned toward me from her bed. The movie continued in the background.

"About my dad? Hate him. About my life? Ambivalent. About our adventure? Surprisingly amused. About your magic man? I'll confess. I want to fuck him. If only to see his eyes roll back in his head like he's some very mortal, very average first year analyst at Goldman Sachs."

Didn't know what to say to that.

"I won't actually have sex with him, Cyur. I just feel that tingly feeling around him, which I was not expecting. It's pretty rare for me. So I must admit it and try to understand it. But I promise after he proves himself a fraud tomorrow, that tingly feeling will evaporate instantly."

"Okay."

"How are YOU feeling?"

"I..." Had to pause, check in with what I was truly feeling. "...I am preparing for disappointment."

"Disappointment that he doesn't have magical powers?"

"No. I'll be more disappointed if he does... and he's still a mirage."

"That's a really weird thing to say. Not weird bad. Like weird cool." Madison sat up, faced me. As if interviewing me. "Okay, sophomore, I need more information on you. Usually I can summarize someone's modus operandi after a five minute conversation. I sure as hell thought I had you pegged after our interview last fall. Including that you'd have a crush on me. But now, after you get me to this farm, and these impressive personalities are here, and this Shepherd and his charming con... and how you held yourself in front of them. Your stumbling, insecure, vulnerability isn't a character flaw you're praying to cure, is it? It's your chosen authentic self. What I mean is that you have done an immense amount of inner self work — for any age, let alone a nineteen year-old — and this you — this wide-eyed innocent, desperately searching for meaning — is the *you* you want to be."

"It is the authentic me... and authenticity is one of the few things we have absolute control over."

"See? Like that answer. That's some pretty profound crap, kid. And now it has an extra layer for me. You're not just saying it because it sounds profound, because it might make a good social media meme. You're saying it because you have thought about it for endless hours, tried to find alternatives, tried to debunk it, but couldn't. It's a hardened profound truth that's earned it's way out of your mouth."

"I think you're incredibly authentic. And much more fun to be around than me."

"One, don't compliment me. Now that I think that you mean everything you say I get even more uncomfortable than when I thought you were saying it in the hope of sleeping with me."

I could say nothing to that.

"And two, yeah, I like to think of myself as authentic. Not on your level I'm realizing, but I'm trying. But me and you arrive at it from opposite directions. I barely think about anything before I say it. I just never censor myself. I have diarrhea of the mouth. But it can come across as brash and fresh and blah blah blah. But your authenticity you work at. You craft every thought in your head for eons before they pass your lips. You're so afraid of saying anything that's not honest you say almost nothing at all."

As if how she was describing me changed how she thought about me, even felt about me, Madison's usually hyper eyes settled into stillness. Then she said, with those eyes and those lips,

"I just had the most insane thought..."

/////////////////

KC glanced up from the printed manuscript Cyur had sent her.

"She wants to kiss him," KC said to herself as she reached for her phone. Who could she call? She couldn't call anyone. No one would answer. "But if she kisses him in that motel room... oh-my-gosh, if she kisses him..."

KC was the one that told Cyur about Shepherd. KC should have been the one in Indiana with Cyur. She should have been the one in that motel room. So why would Cyur want her to read about what had happened there? Cyur was many things, but he was not cruel and he did not send these pages just to prove he had moved on.

And if he didn't send KC this manuscript for that reason, Cyur must have a much bigger reason he did.

# 8

# THE MOTEL, PART TWO

"CYUR..."MADISON said.

"Yes?"

"Usually, when someone says, '*I just had the most insane thought*', and then they pause, you're supposed to ask, 'What?' As in, 'what is this most insane thought you just had?'."

"Sorry."

"Jesus."

"Sorry for saying sorry."

"Americans make fun of Canadians for saying sorry so much. But you'd put any Canadian to shame."

I didn't say I'm sorry. Just stared at Madison. Like I had been doing in the car. But this time she stared back. Two arm lengths separated our beds.

"Cyur..." she said. Soft. Open. Yearning.

"Is it okay if I go to sleep?" I asked. Nervous. Awkward. But honest.

"Ha!"

"I'm sorry."

"Oh, kid... maybe you know what you're doing after all. Yes, yes, go to sleep. Big day tomorrow."

"Good night, Madison." I turned away from her, counting breaths until I fell asleep. One thousand three hundred and eighty-eight I believe.

I DREAMED OF MY DOG. Flame. Asleep on the end of my bed. Curled in the nook of my feet. She never disturbed me. She never let me feel alone.

"CYUR..." a whisper. She's closer than before. I turned to find Madison slipping under the covers of my twin bed. Neither of us are big framed but even so it's impossible for us to lay side by side without falling off. She lifts my arm, slides under it and lays her head on my chest. "Is this okay?"

"It's okay."

"I should have asked before I did it. I'm not going to kiss you or anything. But do you ever just want to be close to someone?"

"Yes," I said.

"I sound so creepy. Am I creepy?"

"No."

"Yes, I am. You have a crush on me and I'm taking advantage of it. But you also think you're in love with me and when a guy thinks they're in love with someone they never want to have sex with them. They just want to hold them. And be near them. And I want to be held. And I'm taking advantage of that. So that's why I'm a creep."

"Madison, I like being close to you. So you're not taking advantage of me."

"You're too good a person for me. I've always been bored by good guys. But I'm realizing those are my character flaws not yours."

"You cannot make yourself attracted to someone you're not attracted to. Just like you cannot make yourself not attracted to someone you are."

"I bet you wish you weren't attracted to me."

"I realize that my chances of creating a true romantic bond with you are very small."

"As small as Shepherd truly being magical?"

"Smaller than even that."

"Why do you want his powers to be real?"

I couldn't answer that. Not quickly.

She filled the silence, "Wouldn't you rather it was you who had real powers?"

"Do you wish you had powers?" I asked.

"Sure. Yeah. I'd start out using my powers for good, but then I'd use them out of boredom and then rage and spite. World is better off without a supernatural Madison. You'd be the better choice. You'd be a good god, Cyur."

"Madison, I..." but I couldn't finish my thought.

"You're really not going to try and kiss me, are you?"

"Madison..." I started again.

This time she didn't fill the silence. Her breath turned heavy. I twisted my head ever so to find her asleep. Cheek against my chest, legs entwined in mine. She stayed there the rest of the night. I never fell back asleep.

9

## THE SILVERADO CONFESSION

**WHEN MADISON BEGAN** to stir at 8:38 am, I untangled myself from her, stood, took another shower then wrote in my laptop on the empty bed.

I thought of KC as I wrote. I thought maybe I'd share this new book with her. Even if our romance was not meant to be, there were things only KC could understand.

**IT TOOK** Madison another hour to fully wake. She didn't say anything. She couldn't look at me. She stayed inside the bathroom for over thirty minutes without ever turning on the shower.

Upon exit, she exploded with, "Fuck, I just tried to find an Uber and there's not one —"

"Apple is waiting in the parking lot for us," I said.

"Shepherd texted us this morning offering a ride. I accepted."

"But that means we have to go straight back to the farm. I don't want to sit around for hours until the food and then more until the puppet show." Her eyes darted between floor, ceiling, walls, the bed. Anywhere but me.

"I'll ask her if we can go into town for a coffee before going to the farm."

She spun her back to me. "No coffee, but yes. Great. I'll pack up."


APPLE SAT behind the wheel of an oversized Silverado pick-up. It dwarfed her, like a kid pretending to drive. I slid into the passenger seat. "Madison will be out in a few minutes."

"Great," she said, gazing ahead. The labored warmth from last night was gone. Today she was ice. Ready to shatter.

"Thank you for coming to get us."

"It's my job."

"How long have you worked for Shepherd?"

She laughed, stopped, laughed again, only to then crack. Her head fell against the steering wheel. Tiny tears dotted the corner of one eye.

"I'm sorry," I said.

"Since you're sort of the only one at the farm today that isn't some sort of illuminati, since you're average like me, can I confess something?"

"Of course."

"You can't tell anyone. Shepherd made me swear I would never say anything."

"Of course," I said.

"Shepherd was my boyfriend. When he was normal. He was cute, even handsome — but not gorgeous like now — and he was a bit chubby, not chubby, just a normal face, not the face of a model. He was funny and silly and I loved him and he loved me. He was so smart. He knew he was. But one of those smart guys that's a bit frustrated at the world for not realizing how smart he is. And then I broke up with him because he couldn't hold a job and I was twenty-three and girls from Indiana need to be thinking about husbands at twenty-three... and he went to Chicago. And went on a bender. He texted me he loved me. And the text had that air of he wasn't going to be long for this earth. I raced to Chicago, tracking him by his phone, and found him in a north side police station. I bailed him out and asked him to marry me. And he said yes and for like an hour we were the happiest we've ever been. But on the drive back, he got sick. Like really sick. And he puked for an hour inside a Taco Bell bathroom. But when he came out, his face had thinned. Dramatically. Changed. It glowed. And I thought he was going to die but he insisted he felt great. I found the nearest hospital anyway. But as we pulled into the parking lot, he created one of those stupid lights... and I thought it was a trick and yelled at him but then he did it again, but this time made the light dance over my face. It was so romantic. Like he had placed a thousand tiny stars on my nose. He said I love you. I remember because it was the last time he said it. Then he spent months in his mom's apartment in Indianapolis. And he would come over every week or so to show me a new magic trick. And every time he would show up, he would be better looking — he looked like a whole new person — and he was gaining confidence, and charm, and I ached so badly for him. He would spend the night. Holding my hand the whole time. And I love how he held my hand so much. I slept so well when he was over. But he never kissed me anymore. He never had sex with me again. He told me we couldn't get married. I should have left. But he begged to be my friend. And how could I leave him now? He was like a real life Harry Potter! And he loved me! I know he did. And so eventually I just said I'd help him with whatever he had planned. Be his manager or assistant or whatever. And he said okay. I wish he didn't let me. But I stayed because I was sure he would someday lose his powers and go back to being just a normal boy that loved me."

By the end, Apple was sobbing. I let her breaths slow. Then said, "That's incredibly hard. And completely understandable why you stayed."

"You're in love with Madison, aren't you?"

"I have never been with Madison like you were with Shepherd, so my feelings for her have not matured like yours. But I definitely wish I could explore a romantic relationship with her."

"But you know Shepherd is going to make her love him. You'll never have a chance."

"If Madison falls in love with Shepherd, then that is what is meant to be. I'll be hurt, but I'll mend with time."

"No, she won't fall in love with him. Shepherd will use his powers. Madison will think it's love but really it's just his magic."

"I would like to believe, even if Shepherd's powers are very real, that he would not or could not use them to make someone feel something they don't naturally feel."

"Then you have no idea who Henry really is."

"Is Henry his real name?"

Apple's face flushed white. "You can't know that... here comes Madison... Cyur, you can't say anything or even think it... you don't understand, he can read thoughts..."

Madison opened up the back door, tossed her bag along the seat and then slid in to find a red faced Apple and a silent me.

"Oh, boy, what did you do, sophomore?"

"I..." I started —

But Apple perked up, smiled big, and said, "My boyfriend broke up with me last night. And I needed to sob to the first person I saw. Lucky for you Cyur came out first."

"Well, Apple, even though you're a couple years older than me I'm gonna be obnoxious and give you some dating advice: there are infinite men in the world. They are, every last one, disposable. There is only one you... and you, beautiful, are priceless." As Madison finished, Apple burst into another sobbing fit. Madison mumbled, "I actually thought my advice was pretty good. I'm sorry."

"It was... it's just I have to hate you and what you said was amazing and that makes it hard to hate you."

"Why do you have to hate me?!"

Apple sucked in a calm breath, wiped her tears. She winked at me for our shared secret, then said, "Oh, you know, you're younger, prettier, richer, and smarter. I had no choice."

"Younger yes, richer yes, but the rest is incredibly

subjective. But it's a visual fact you have the better boobs and butt."

Apple laughed again, then turned on the truck. "Ready?"

"Oh," I said, "I forgot to ask if we could go into town first."

"Shepherd wants..." Apple began, a chill coursing through her yet again.

Madison said, "Just need a Starbucks and a shot of small town Americana before your boss's big day makes me forget everything else. Oh, and alcohol."

"Yes, okay. That makes sense. West Woods is nice. Sort of. There's no Starbucks. But you'll like the cafe. And Dusty will love you."

"Dusty. What a name. Let's do it! Another mini Madison and Cyur adventure, this time with guest star Apple!"

On the way, I considered all Apple had said. Especially her insistence that Shepherd could read minds. Not just read but influence minds. Something both Jamelle and Katarina had hinted at last night.

For reasons I can't explain this frightened me more than whether he could open a door to the afterlife.

# 10

# THE LAST COFFEE

DOWNTOWN WEST WOODS, Indiana, was a block long. Even that was generous. A hundred meters of store fronts on each side of a badly paved main street. Half the store fronts boarded, either for winter or forever, the rest closed for the holiday. The only two open were the gas station and the Hill-Billie Cafe.

"Billie was his wife, who died in a snowmobile accident," Apple noted.

Madison laughed. "Oh, my god, I can't believe I laughed at that. I'm truly an awful person. I'll tip Dusty excessively as penance." As we stepped out of the truck, Apple stayed behind. Madison insisted, "Listen, beautiful, you have to join us."

"I *have* to re-do my make-up," Apple said, taking out a bag from her purse.

"No, you don't. You're naturally perfect. But I

know you're not gonna budge, so I'm buying you Dusty's fanciest latte."

"I still have to hate you."

"I hate me, too, so I get it." Madison spun toward the front door. I followed.

THE LINE inside was an impressive five deep. "Don't let me get a coffee," Madison said.

"Okay?"

"So this boyfriend of Apple was Shepherd, right?"

"It is not my story to share."

"I should have known you're not a gossip. Ugh. Oh, kid, are we even the same species?"

"I think so."

"Ha! You're even more awkward today." At the register a thick middle-aged man with small eyes and a big beard welcomed us with a,

"Welcome to real America, city dwellers," he said with a not-so-toothy grin.

"We're that obvious, eh, Dusty?" Madison said.

"You all smell the same: expensive cooking oil."

"Fascinating. Give us three of your fanciest lattes as long as they have three espresso shots and matching sugar levels." Madison turned to me. "I'm ordering for you. If you're gonna be more awkward, I'm gonna be more obnoxious."

"But you said no coffee for you —"

"Shhh. Dusty, ignore him."

Dusty said, "Three White Chocolate Dusty specials."

"Perfect," Madison said as she handed over her card. "Say, Dusty, what do you know about the old Cottage Christmas tree farm near here?"

"The Christmas tree farm closed down in '08. It was owned by the Quayle family. Yeah, that Quayle family. All I know now is that young Indianapolis boy bought it six months ago and does some witchcraft crap out there. I hear he sacrifices virgins, so stay away from there, city girl."

"Well, I'm very *very* safe then, if you know what I mean. But thank you for the insider information. And thank you for making the world a little less boring today."

Dusty, bored with us, looked to the next customer, "Ron, save me."

APPLE WAS ONLY half way through her make-up operation, so Madison put her latte in the center console and said, "Me and the kid are gonna walk around the town. Literally, we will do a three hundred meter circle and cover the entire thing. You keep doing you."

Twenty steps away from the Silverado, Madison said, "Okay, Cyur. This is probably the last time we will ever be alone."

I stiffened.

"I feel profound shame for being creepy last night and yet equally devastating rejection. If you had been a normal kind of pathetic and just slept with me, I would have never talked to you again either. So it was a lose-lose, kid. I'm sorry. You had some romantic fantasy roadmap and yet it was always gonna be a crash and burn. Lesson here is don't ever develop crushes on insecure narcissists! No matter how sexy or smart or hilarious we might be."

I smiled.

"Okay. Thank you for laughing at my joke. Or smiling. Or whatever it is you just did. You got about two hundred more steps before we get back to the truck so give me your big speech. Since I'll never know if you're secretly an immortal lover who inspires a strange novella when I'm fifty, you have to make the next sentences out of your mouth make me think of you the night before I marry some billionaire asshole who cheats on me with our nanny. I'm jumping time frames but you get it."

"It's okay."

"What's okay?"

"It's okay. Don't worry about me."

"I'm not worried about you! *You* made me feel creepy and rejected!"

"I'm sorry."

"Oh, my god, a normal sleazy dude would have slept with me. And a normal self righteous dork would be dramatically pitching his romantic vision for our lives together. But you. You got an 'it's okay' and 'I'm sorry'."

"I always feel seen when I'm in your presence, Madison."

"Huh?"

"I am stating the most non-debatable reason I like you. You see me. Whether you see the shy me like most of the past year, or the expressive one like last night. Both are me. And you see them both."

"Seen? Okay. And I guess thank you? But that's what I do for you. Your romantic pitch has to be why you're my soul mate or whatever."

"I don't think I believe in soul mates."

"My god, you're terrible at this."

"I'm sorry."

"NO MORE 'I'M SORRIES'!"

I said nothing.

"I yelled. I don't even know why I yelled."

"I feel seen when around you. How do you feel when you're around me?"

"Creepy and rejected. We've been over this."

"Those aren't good feelings. I understand why you don't want to see me again."

"Are you a robot?"

I said nothing.

"Oh, kid, I don't know... Why do I call you kid? I've never called anyone else 'kid' in my life. Maybe I'm Han Solo and you're Luke Skywalker. That would mean you're a Jedi. Are you a Jedi, Cyur?"

"My mother never let me watch Star Wars."

"That explains *so* much," Madison said, then stopped. So I did, too. Turned and faced her. She looked into my eyes for the first time since last night. "Truth?" she asked.

"Always the best option."

"Yes, I feel creepy and rejected when I think about last night. But what do I feel now? What is the dominant thing you made me feel the past twenty-four hours?"

I waited.

"Crap..."

"What?" I asked.

"Seen... seen. You make me feel seen, too, Cyur. *Seen.* It sounded small when you said it. But now that I'm saying it, now that I'm feeling it, it feels vital. Honestly you might be the only person who has ever made me feel this way."

"Thank you."

"I'm thanking YOU!"

"Thank you for expressing your truth. Truth is vulnerable. Vulnerable is beautiful. And beautiful is beautiful to witness. So thank you."

She laughed. "You really are a robot. Programed to speak like a Jane Austen pixie dream boy."

"I don't know what that means."

"That's okay. We have to go. Our ride is hailing us and we need to run to the gas station for alcohol before going back to the farm," she said. I turned to see Apple beckoning from the truck fifty meters away. When I turned back, Madison was a step closer. Eyes into mine. She said, "If I was truly a creep, I'd kiss you. If you weren't an alien, you'd kiss me. But since I'm afraid of rejection and you're afraid of being human, let's just stare at each other intimately for a moment. Hold our gaze until our nerves or the universe stops us."

Our eyes enlarged and then, slowly, and then, immensely, fused. Energy poured from her into me, penetrated my thoughts and emotions, and then birthed new energy that flowed into her. And then she did the same. Back and forth. Our energies intercoursing as if naked bodies, as if bare souls. We stood alone, close, on an empty street in an empty town. Our worlds had shrunk to the small space between us. And the infinite space inside us.

. . .

MAYBE IT WAS A MINUTE. Maybe it was ten. But Apple began yelling our names. Madison broke her eyes away from mine, looked toward our escort back to the mission, and yelled, "Coming!" Then she looked back at me, her hard shell once more shed, if only for her to say, "That was better than any speech. Better than any sex. Better than any kiss. But it will still be the last time we are ever alone."

11:44 AM

BACK ON THE TOILET. COFFEE IS MY DEVIL!

APPLE HATES ME FOR THINKING I'M GONNA STEAL SHEPHERD FROM HER WHEN I'M REALLY GOING TO DESTROY HIM FOR BOTH OUR SAKES. SHE STILL DID LET ME USE HER PRIVATE BATH-ROOM. I OWE HER. THIS IS NOT A SMELL THAT OTHER PEOPLE SHOULD KNOW I CAN PRODUCE.

I SHOULD PROBABLY TYPE SOMETHING ABOUT CYUR. IF I DON'T MAYBE I'LL BE ABLE TO FORGET ANY OF THE CRINGY OR PROFOUND EXPERIENCES WITH HIM SINCE LAST NIGHT.

BUT THEN I'D BE A BAD WRITER AND A WORSE PERSON SO FUCK IT.

ONE) SHOULD NEVER HAVE GOTTEN INTO BED WITH HIM. CAN YOU IMAGINE IF I WAS A DUDE, A SENIOR, HIS EDITOR, AND HE WAS SOME WIDE EYE SOPHOMORE CHICK? THE #METOO ARMY WOULD LINE ME UP FOR THE FIRING SQUAD AND RIGHTFULLY SO.

TWO) I SHOULD SLOW DOWN WITH THE JUDGEMENTS. WITH EVERYONE. BUT ESPE-CIALLY WITH CYUR. I PIGEON-HOLED HIM AS AN INSECURE, HOPELESS ROMANTIC. WHICH HE STILL MIGHT BE! BUT HE'S ALSO MORE. AND THE MORE MIGHT BE MORE THAN I CAN IMAGINE RIGHT NOW. I DISMISSED HIM, THEN I TRIED TO SLEEP WITH HIM, AND THEN WE HAVE EYE SEX TO END ALL EYE SEX, AND NOW I WANT TO DISMISS HIM AGAIN. WHY? AM I GONNA EVER BRING HIM TO NEW YORK AND SAY, "HEY DAD, HERE'S MY BOYFRIEND. HE'S A DORKY, AVERAGE STUDENT, AVERAGE WRITER. HE COMES FROM NO MONEY, HE HAS NO GOOD JOB PROSPECTS, BUT HE MAKES ME FEEL SEEN WHICH YOU'VE NEVER DONE." HA. NO. OBVI-OUSLY NO. RIGHT? RIGHT.

THREE) Cuz there always has to be three and as a counterpoint to two... before I die, and probably before I get married, and maybe even before the end of the day, I should look him in the eyes again. See if our eyes want to make love again. See if it's him, not Shepherd, that is magical in the only way that matters.

# 11

# DRINKS & THOUGHTS

MADISON RACED into the house when we got back to the farm then upstairs. Apple followed, carrying the purchased wine, vodka, and tequila. After throwing away the coffee I never sipped because my stomach cannot handle caffeine or dairy, let alone both at the same time, I wandered back toward the great room we talked in last night. The couches had been turned to form a semi-circle alongside the fireplace instead of toward it. The room was now centered with a reclaimed wood dining table. Four cameras on tripods surrounded it. The last a reminder that Shepherd not only promised to perform a miracle in front of us here in this room but in front of thousands, perhaps millions, online.

Apple veered toward the kitchen, dropping the

drinks on the large soapstone island before trading in her assistant duties for cooking duties.

Jamelle, Katarina, Nikki, and William stood close together by the fireplace, coffees in hand. The zeal in their eyes from last night had cooled. Their drooping shoulders and easy yawns suggested they were still waking up even though it was almost noon.

"Cyur!" Nikki exclaimed as I neared. She stepped toward me, hugging me as if we were old friends. "Sorry," she said, "It's just that I slept so well last night I don't know what to do with my body."

"We were just discussing that," Jamelle said, "How none of us can remember sleeping as long and as deeply. No matter what today holds, there *is* something special about this farm."

Katarina added, "I'll help Shepherd turn it into a bed and breakfast if being the next messiah doesn't work out."

They all laughed. Except William. He didn't share the others' joy. His gaze focused on me, intensifying with every second until I asked, "Did you not sleep well, William?"

"Oh, I did... but I don't trust it." The other three laughed. To their bemusement, a now grumbling William said, "Oh, I'm very serious. Why *did* we sleep so well? Did he put something in our sparkling waters last night? Did he visit us in our dreams? Steal small pieces of our soul that will make it easier to manipulate us later?"

Nikki laughed. The others held back in the face of William's graveness. Nikki said, "Oh, I... you're being serious about being serious, aren't you? Sorry. Forgot about your... beliefs. I need more coffee. Or maybe it's time to try alcohol. Because that sleep was so good my brain might be telling me no amount of coffee will wake it up ever again." Nikki drifted off toward the kitchen.

"Did you sleep well?" Katarina asked me.

"A little," I said, in that I slept very little.

"Shepherd said we could stay here for the weekend. I never planned to. But after last night's sleep, I'm somehow tempted. Maybe you and Madison could spend the night tonight..." Jamelle said.

"Maybe," I said, though I thought this unlikely for many reasons.

"Why *are* you here?" William asked, unable to hold back his agitation at my presence any longer. The night at the farm had left the others — Nikki, Jamelle, and Katarina — basking in a blissful haze. As if free of the burdens they brought to this farm. Free of the angst that inspired their answers in last night's conversation. But William's eyes couldn't focus. His body swayed. Like he had been drugged and didn't know it. And not knowing was the worst part. It left him feeling paranoid.

"I'm here," I started, "looking for larger truths just like you, William."

"Yes, yes, I know that," William spat, "but why are YOU here? Why were you allowed here? Why did Shepherd allow you here? You shouldn't be allowed here. Everyone else has a purpose here for Shepherd. What's your purpose?"

"William," Jamelle said, "Let's keep our words kind. Our hearts open..."

"Cyur, William doesn't mean it," Katarina said though it was clear to all of us William meant every word.

"It's okay. I understand."

William lunged at me. Stumbled really. "It's not okay... who ARE you? WHO ARE YOU?!"

Jamelle took William under the arm before he could get closer to me. "I'm going to take him for some fresh air." They exited out the kitchen glass slider onto a back porch.

Katarina said, "William was actually saying the same things we were until you arrived... I don't mean it's your fault..."

"It's okay. I understand."

"Ooh," Katarina said as Madison stepped into the

room. "Do you think Madison would do an interview with me?"

"I don't know."

"I'll ask her. She likes men?"

I said nothing.

"Bad question. Sorry. I have a girlfriend. I love my girlfriend. And Madison is way too young for me. But there's something amazing about her. Other-worldly. Why am I saying this to you? I'm sorry, Cyur. Maybe you do cause people to say strange stuff. I'm going to go now. Please forget everything I just said."

Katarina and Madison crossed from opposite sides of the great room to gather around Nikki at the kitchen island. Each poured themselves a drink, then spun around to face the room as if three friends surveying a party for dancing partners. Except Jamelle was outside with William, Shepherd had still not made his entrance, and I stood by myself, more awkward than ever, by the fireplace.

I waved at them. Like a pimply twelve year-old boy might wave at three famous actresses.

Madison yelled across the room, "I would tell you to relax and have a drink but I bet you don't drink either."

"It makes me feel —"

"— sick," Madison finished my sentence. Then unleashed frustration coated in joviality, "Everything that's bad for you makes you feel sick. No junk food, no pot, no alcohol, no sex. Maybe you're not a good person by choice, kid. Maybe you're only good because your body won't let you be bad."

Nikki and Katarina laughed. But Madison's face faded into shame the moment the words left her mouth. I was an easy person to make fun of and Madison hated herself for choosing easy.

Yesterday her father abandoned her yet again, last night our connection left her more confused than comforted, and today she might witness a miracle that would break her heart as much as heal it. I understood why her anxiety let her say what she did. *I'm sorry,* she tried to say without words.

*It's okay,* I said without words in return.

"I said no more okays," Madison responded aloud as if she had read my thoughts.

# 12

# THE FIRST (MAGIC) ACT

THOUGH SHEPHERD still had not descended from his room upstairs, Apple invited us to sit down.

Eight plate settings. A name in calligraphy at each. Jamelle and Nikki on one side. Katarina and William on the other. Apple and I next to one another at the end, out of view from the cameras. At the head of the table: Madison's name next to Shepherd as if she was the co-host. Or his wife.

As Apple brought the food to the table, everyone stood behind their chair. Except Madison. She tried to switch her seat assignment with Apple.

Apple intercepted her: "Oh, no. No, no, no. It's very important you sit next to Shepherd."

"I'll be more comfortable down here, out of the camera's view."

The panic on Apple's face was severe. "No, no. I'm

sorry. I don't think you understand. He can't do this without you. I mean, he's doing it for you. I mean... it's your mom."

Madison looked to me for guidance. I said, "Do you mind if I whisper something to you?"

She laughed. "Only you would ask..."

I waited.

"Yes, Cyur, *yes*. Whisper away."

I leaned close, my lips inches from her ear. "I am concerned that if Shepherd's powers prove real, you will have a difficult time..."

Madison twisted backwards until her mouth was now at my ear. She whispered, "When he proves to be a fraud, you're going to prove to be a fool and you're gonna really wish you kissed me when you had the chance." She pulled away from me, circled back to the head of the table and waited behind her assigned seat. Next to Shepherd's. A queen waiting for her king. As I noticed the record button on all the cameras glow red, a voice said:

"Please, sit..." We all turned. At the entrance, under the archway into the great room, stood Shepherd. We collectively, silently, were awed by the sight of him. Last night his jeans and button-down understated his good looks and charm. But today, adorned in a bright-white, medieval frock with an exaggerated pointed collar and white emeralds lined from his neck to mid-thigh, Shepherd now had the visual presentation of what he aspired to be: a spiritual leader for a new age. Any man less confident, less beautiful, less ready for this moment might have left Madison and others giggling at the audaciousness of his outfit. Instead, his clothes, his energy, his mission all aligned into a collective sensation: Shepherd Cottage would prove to be everything he promised to be.

No one sat. Instead we watched as he crossed toward us. It was akin to watching royalty — or the pope — join you for dinner. Madison could not help but swoon. Nor could the other guests. Even I fell under his spell. Watching Madison watch him, I knew — if Shepherd fulfilled all he claimed — that her attention, and likely her love, would be forever his.

"WELL," Madison said, nervous, as Shepherd stepped behind the chair next to her, "I feel underdressed."

The table laughed. I with it. A perfect release of our tension. Shepherd again asked, "Please, sit," and this time we all did as told.

THE FOOD WAS classic American Thanksgiving. A big turkey, heavy gravy, rich stuffing, creamy everything else. My weak stomach allowed for nothing but undressed salad and unbuttered bread. The conversation returned to how satisfying the night's sleep was in the house. Jamelle, Nikki, and Katarina over-thanking Shepherd to the point of idolization.

"How do you do it?" William Weigel asked.

"Do what, William?" Shepherd's cadence was slower today. More measured. It kept the table calm. We were children that felt safe in the presence of an esteemed adult.

William, less sure of his earlier conspiracies, said, "How did you make it so easy to sleep... I'm almost fifty... I usually get up to pee at least twice during the night..."

Katarina and Nikki tried to contain their bemusement.

William, embarrassed, said, "I mean... when I woke it was after nine and I haven't slept past six in a decade..."

"I'm so happy you slept well here, William," Shepherd said. "I'm hoping whatever peace you felt here last night, you will feel every night now. I hope — " He nodded toward the cameras, "People watching will begin to feel that same peace, too."

Madison had grown more uncomfortable with every compliment the others gave Shepherd. Her eyes — and her body — could not hide her magnetic attraction to him. But her mind fought it with all it had. She said, "So, Shepherd... the sophomore says you renamed yourself Shepherd as part your hero origin story. That true?"

Shepherd smiled. Nothing would phase him today. He was so sure of himself and his destiny.

Apple leaned toward me, whispered, "He's more beautiful today than I've ever seen. How can someone get more beautiful every day?" I didn't nod. But I couldn't argue it either. I didn't know him like Apple did, but Shepherd's physical appearance *had* evolved from the first video he posted. He was always a handsome man but now he was beautiful. Almost inhumanly beautiful. Beautiful in the way a perfect work of art is. You feel the beauty inside you.

Shepherd took Madison's hand in his own, held it on the table as he nodded toward the cameras. "Madison, many people watching know who you are. But they do not understand why you are who you are. Do you want to tell them?"

"If I knew why I was who I am, I would save a lot of money and time on therapy... and self-medication." She raised her drink.

"Can I attempt an analysis?" Shepherd asked with a humble aura that somehow weaved flawlessly with his impenetrable confidence.

"Why not," Madison said. "The sophomore over

there did a half way decent job yesterday so you'll have to do better than him to impress me."

Shepherd took a moment to look in my direction. It was only a second, but I could describe it as nothing less than he was trying to pull something out of me. Maybe what I had said about Madison's relationship with her father yesterday? Maybe Apple was right about his ability to enter other's minds.

But after that brief moment with me, Shepherd returned to Madison. Squeezing her hand again. This eased her. As if his touch alone could release her tension. "Madison, you were born into immense wealth. You will leave this earth with immense wealth. Not millions of dollars. Billions. More money than 99.999% of every human to ever live and who will ever live will ever have. So, for almost everyone watching, here and online, they cannot fathom having any concerns that cannot be solved with money. Can money buy happiness? Debatable. But it definitely can buy joy — joy from material things, travel, experiences. Can money buy love? Debatable. But it can buy endless opportunities to meet the most inter-esting and gorgeous humans on earth. But you, Madison, do not wake up looking for happiness or love, do you?"

Madison didn't respond. Yet hung on Shepherd's every word.

"You, Madison, are looking for meaning. *Why* were

you born with all this money and power yet it means nothing to you? *Why* were you born to a father obsessed with making sure the whole world knows who he is yet does not care if his own daughter does? *Why* did your beautiful and brilliant mother take her own life when she had a daughter whose life had barely begun?"

The mention of her mother tightened Madison. She wanted to at once shrink and explode. But Shepherd's hand in hers kept her still.

"You asked about my name. True, I was not born with the name Shepherd. I gave myself this name when I realized that these powers given to me had to be used for a purpose greater than my own glory. I had to have a name that felt humble enough for anyone to approach but have enough meaning that everyone knew why I was here. That's why you're here, Madison. You're here searching for meaning. You're here in Indiana searching for *why*. You're here to discover that when you stop trying to prove there's no such thing as magic you will find magic all around you."

SHEPHERD THEN WAVED his free hand above him. At once, the food, our plates, and the silverware levitated off the table. The guests' jaws literally dropped in wonder. Smiling. Giddy. Like children watching fireworks. Shepherd squeezed Madison's hand once more, then waved his other again... and all of us at the table, along with the chairs we sat in, levitated off the ground just as the food had risen from the table. Smiles disappeared. Childlike wonder transformed into cosmic shock.

We were floating. Floating above the ground. As if the rules of gravity no longer applied to us. As if those rules had been re-written by our host.

Each of the guests could no longer deny what they had all come here to disprove: Shepherd Cottage had supernatural powers none had imagined possible.

All that was left to discover was what he planned to do with these powers.

13

## THE FEAR OF WHAT MIGHT BE

SHEPHERD THEN EASED us back to the floor (and the food, plates, and silverware to the table) with the same gentle, invisible strength he had lifted us off it.

To the cameras, he said, "Please allow us ten minutes before I begin what I know you are here to witness. I need to regain my strength and I'm sure my guests need a moment as well." Then he tapped the air and all four camera lights went dark.

Jamelle laughed. A deep belly laugh. A laugh that spoke what words could not. Nikki rubbed her fingers against her forehead as if replaying what had just happened. William remained frozen in place. Perhaps his mind still could not comprehend what had transpired. Katarina was the first to speak: "Holy-holy, holy, HOLY shit!"

"What she said," Nikki followed, then laughed with the same profound release as Jamelle.

Katarina leapt from the table, phone to mouth: "Did you see it? It was real. It was *so* real. Start a recording. Let's FaceTime once I'm outside. I need to comment on it and then be ahead of whatever Shepherd does next." Katarina then sealed herself out on the deck, beginning her own video. She was both reporter and participant and she knew it was vital she played both roles well.

Nikki and Jamelle retreated to the kitchen island, pouring themselves drinks just to have something to do as they began the impossible task of deciding what all this might mean.

MADISON HAD NOT MOVED. Unlike William's rigid tension, Madison's skin quivered, her eyes danced. Suggesting a mind and soul that was trying to re-write all she thought was possible. Both re-write what was behind her. And, most importantly, what might be in front of her in the very near future.

Shepherd, sensing her vulnerable state, said, "Is it okay that I let your hand go? I promise to hold it again when we take our next step together."

Madison nodded. Shepherd let go. She slumped into her seat as if she no longer had the strength to hold herself up. Shepherd caught her. I leapt up, rushed around the table, and supported her from the other side.

To me, Shepherd asked, "You care about her deeply, don't you?"

I didn't answer. Didn't know how to authentically. I did care for Madison. But if I said yes then I would be speaking to my mostly innocent romantic crush. If I said no, I would be denying how vital her presence in my life this past year had been.

To my silence, Shepherd said, "I understand, Cyur. I promise I'll take care of her." He spoke as if he knew they were meant to be together. As if Shepherd knew the bond he just shared with Madison was the beginning of something bigger than I could imagine. "Can you stay with her a few moments? I need to get some water and answer questions from the others."

As he stepped away, my eyes fell on Apple as she cleared the plates from the table. *Told you*, she mouthed. Told me what? Oh, yes. That Shepherd would use his magic to make Madison fall in love with him. That's not how I felt. If Madison did fall for Shepherd, no one would question why. Least of all me. Shepherd had beauty, kindness, and talent. His talent just happened to be supernatural.

"Kid?" Madison whispered. Not whispered. Her voice was hoarse. Dry. Exhausted. As if she was the one that just waved her hand and floated us all off the ground.

"Yes, Madison?"

"He's really a god, isn't he?"

"I don't know if that's the right word. But he does have powers no one else appears to have."

"Cyur..."

"Yes, Madison?"

"Why am I so tired?"

"This is a lot to process."

"He's gonna do it for real, isn't he?"

"Bring back your mom from the dead?"

"Yes. He's gonna really do it, isn't he?"

"I think so."

"I don't want to see her."

"Let's tell him not to do it then."

"I can't."

"I'll tell him."

"No, I don't want to see her.... But I can't *not* see her... if there's even a chance, I have to... I have to see her... I have to ask her why..."

"Okay."

She smiled. "I liked that okay."

"Okay."

"You know why?"

"Why?"

"Because I know what your okays mean now. This

one meant, *I understand why you don't want to see your mom, Madison, but I also understand why you have to see your mom, but I ALSO understand why I will stop Shepherd if it's too much for you.*

"I said all that in one 'okay'?" I held her hand. It did not ease her angst like Shepherd holding it. But it eased mine.

"Yes. You did. See? Your okays need subtitles. Or just someone really brilliant like me to interpret them."

"Madison..." I started.

"What?"

I couldn't say it. I couldn't speak this one truth. It was not the right place. It was not the right time. Perhaps not the right lifetime.

# 14

# THE MOMENTS BEFORE

WHEN MADISON SETTLED, I helped Apple finish clearing the table. As I stacked dishes, I overheard some of Shepherd's conversation with Nikki and Jamelle. He was patient with both their excitement and bewilderment.

My years long search for someone, anyone, that could restore my faith in a higher power felt like it was on the cusp of being rewarded. I even considered texting KC a thank you for sending me the link to Shepherd's work. Instead I sent my unfinished book. Just in case it remained unfinished.

Once the dishes were done and Katarina retuned inside, Shepherd moved in front of the fireplace and announced, "Can I have Jamelle, Nikki, Katarina, and William sit down on the two couches. Madison, if you could stand beside me."

"What about Cyur?" Madison asked.

Shepherd explained, "It would be best for Cyur to remain in the kitchen. He can watch. But it can be only the five of you around the fireplace and in the cameras' view."

Madison stood up from the dining table but kept one hand on it even as the other four took their places on the couches facing Shepherd.

"Madison, please." Shepherd pointed again next to him.

Madison looked toward me. I did not feel slighted being told my place was in the kitchen. I knew I did not hold the same importance as the others. But I also knew Madison was nervous about what might happen. I had witnessed her panic attack in the car yesterday and could sense her body on the edge of another.

"Madison..." Shepherd started to ask again but sensed at once she was not ready. "Fine. I'll start with you standing there. Before I turn on the cameras, let me explain what is about to happen. And why it's about to happen. And what will happen after that."

"So you can also predict the future?" Nikki asked, half joking.

Shepherd pinched his lips, suggesting *yes, he could predict the future...* and so much more. "I have tried to slowly prepare all of you — and my online audience — for what lies ahead. But even so, I have sympathy for what I am asking each of you to witness. Not only witness, but then report, defend, expand. Last night, after I left for bed, I know some of you questioned whether my powers were real. That has been answered. Others wondered if I used my powers to inspire you to come to Indiana."

Jamelle and Katarina shared a knowing glance.

"The answer is yes. I did in the same way the sun inspires the flowers to turn toward it. For since I first realized I had gifts beyond all other men and women, I have had visions of what will be. Not dreams. Not hopes. Not visions of what could be or should be. Visions of what *will* be. I know how this sounds. I know I am shedding some of my humbleness in these last few moments before the world sees what I truly am. But it's important to know you are all here with a very important purpose. For one of my clearest visions was of the one we are about to have. Jamelle and Katarina on that couch, William and Nikki on that one. And Madison holding my hand as I opened a portal to the afterlife..."

*A portal to the afterlife.*

Everyone, for the first time, accepted this would happen.

To that, Shepherd explained, "You can sense just like I that the strength of my superpowers are a magnitude greater today than yesterday. You do not need to know why this is. But you should know my vision of the future always told me this Thanksgiving was when my powers would fully bloom. That it was only today, in this moment that will occur moments from now, that I was truly able to open a door to the after-life. Open it and communicate with someone who long ago left this world." Shepherd nodded toward Madison, who steeled as if the nod was a punch. He continued, "When this happens — and it will happen just as all my other visions have happened — there will not simply be a worldwide question of *Who is this Shepherd Cottage with superhuman powers?* Thousands then millions will also see for the first time that there is life after death. And that will change everything. Religions will fall. A new religion will rise. And I will have to guide humanity on how to comprehend all these changes. On how we live in this life and how we will live in the next. I will have to ensure that peace prevails as so many different factions fight for relevance in this new paradigm. And I cannot do it alone. I know I cannot do it alone because in every one of my visions, you five were here today... and you five were by my side in the future. Jamelle to advise me on how to lead. Nikki on how to communicate. Katarina on how to build. And William, I know you have questioned why you are here more than anyone else... you will help me create a bridge between religions of the past and the religion we will all create together."

"Um," Madison raised her hand with an air of mockery, "and am I here just to be the token rich white girl?"

Shepherd smiled. "I know you can sense it, Madison. I know you fight it as well. But we will be partners. Romantic and spiritual partners. Together, we will make sure no one has to doubt their purpose — as you have — on this earth ever again."

A COLLECTIVE SILENCE descended over the room. Shepherd wanted to give everyone a minute to process what he had said. He also knew he had to give time for the inevitable:

"NIKKI," Shepherd said. "Go ahead and say it."

"Say what?"

"What you wanted to say but were afraid to in case everything I just said turns out to be true."

Everyone looked toward her. "Okay. Screw it —" Nikki took a deep breath. "This is all fucking insane."

Everyone laughed. Even Shepherd. The only ones who didn't were Apple and me.

Shepherd said, "Yes. It is. But the world is not

changed by what can be predicted. It does not change with everyone comfortable. It is not changed by average people or average thinking or average ambitions. It changes when it must. It changes to survive right before it's going to destroy itself. And each of you can see it. You can sense the world is angry. It's afraid. It wants to destroy itself to free itself from the anger and pain. But I know I was given these powers to save it. It's my destiny to save the world."

ANOTHER SILENCE. But this time because all eyes were on my raised hand. As if a high school student with a poorly timed question. Shepherd, restraining his impatience, offered, "Cyur, do you have a question that must be answered before we begin?"

I felt incredibly self-conscious, but knew I must risk further embarrassment and ask it. The words stumbled out of my mouth, "How, um, are you so sure of the reasons... I mean, why are you so sure your powers were given to you for a reason?"

"Why else would I possess such special gifts unless I was meant to do special things with these gifts?"

"Maybe you're right," I said, "but, maybe, what if you have powers because you happened to be in Chicago on a random Tuesday and if you had been in, I don't know, Denver instead, someone else would have been in Chicago and gotten the same powers instead of you?"

It pained Shepherd to hold back his agitation. "Cyur, *every* vision I have had since I became super-human has come true. That's not the universe being random, that's the universe aligning for my destiny."

No one could look my way. All too embarrassed for me. Save Madison. She never flinched. I stumbled on with, "But... because you *have* superpowers, don't you think you can *make* things happen that you want to have happen? I mean... sorry, it's just I really admire how confident you are and just want to understand it... but what if your vision of the future is really just a future possibility and you are using your magic to ensure that future possibility occurs?"

All eyes turned to Shepherd. But he could no longer mask his annoyance at my interruption. At my very presence. "Cyur, you're now distracting from everyone else's experience. I'm going to ask you remain quiet until afterwards or I'm going to have to ask you to leave."

I fell silent. Perhaps Shepherd was right. I was just one insecure soul needing very specific questions explored. Someone as self-assured as Shepherd must have reasons I cannot comprehend.

.   .   .

CONFIDENT MY DISRUPTION WAS OVER, Shepherd said, "Madison, come take my hand. Let's open this portal, heal the wound between you and your mother, and then begin the healing for everyone else."

All looked toward her. Despite Shepherd's grand speech of all that was to be, Madison held her ground. Then, looking toward me, she said, "I want Cyur with me."

"What do you mean?"

"I want Cyur by my side as you open the portal. I'll hold your hand. But I want him next to me."

Shepherd hesitated. His words slowed, "When Cyur messaged me yesterday, I leapt at the easiest path to get you here. I thought he would have left by now. I assumed you would send him home. Or something would draw him away. Because he has never been in any of my visions of today. He is never in any of my visions of the future. I cannot risk all the universe has asked us to do for one person."

I said nothing.

Madison pressed, "So if someone is not in your vision, they're not important?"

"You don't trust me," Shepherd stated.

"No. I don't."

"But you will fall in love with me. You are drawn to me right now. On every level that two people can be drawn toward each other."

Madison said, "You are, Shepherd, the most beautiful human I have ever seen. You have powers I still cannot grasp. But you do not lack ego —"

"I cannot apologize for understanding my destiny."

"I know. I get it. My dad will love you."

"I'm not your father, Madison. I will never leave you. I need you almost as much as you need me. If you will just take my hand, we can open the portal and then you will see. You will see everything we can accomplish together. You will finally trust me."

Madison let out a deep breath. "Here's the thing. I was one hundred percent sure you were a fraud. Was as sure as I am that if I have a coffee I'm gonna need a toilet. I was sure right up until you held my hand at the dinner table. Something left me when you did. Maybe it was my doubt. Maybe it was my own autonomy. But when that something left, I knew... I knew you were real. I knew Cyur was right about you. So I know you're going to do it. I know you're going to open a portal to the next world. I know I'm going to see my mom... but I also know enough about visionary people to know that if something gets between them and their vision... between them and their destiny... they will always destroy whatever gets between them. Even if that someone is me."

Shepherd took in a deep breath. He had not been refused in a long time. He was handling it as well as most men like him could. "Madison, I cannot open the portal without you."

"I accept that. I will hold your hand. I just want Cyur next to me."

"He's, um... a kid. You call him a kid. He's not one of us. He's not published. He's not famous. Not important. I don't understand. I'm sorry, Cyur. I don't mean to insult you. But I don't want you getting hurt. And I don't want you disrupting my destiny to save the world."

I did not react.

Madison said, "Here's why. Because Cyur would never say 'my destiny'. As far as any of us know, you're the only one on earth with supernatural powers. So your destiny really might be to save the world. Or destroy it. But Cyur... he's not going to be thinking about saving the world today. He's just going to be thinking about if I'm scared and I need it to stop."

Shepherd's frustration was building. He didn't know how to redirect it.

Sensing a stalemate, Jamelle stood and said, "Shepherd... you have opened my mind to all sorts of new possibilities these past twenty-four hours. You did say you had a vision that I will guide you on how to lead. Well, let me start now. Madison is right. Leaders cannot have visions so narrow that they cannot adapt to new ideas. To new people. You didn't envision Cyur here. But he is here. He has been nothing but vulnerable and patient with all of us. He has not flinched as you questioned his worth. You say you need Madison's hand to open the portal. She needs Cyur. I have studied great spiritual leaders dating back to the ancients. The great ones always listened to their disciples. And that's what we are, right? We are. I accept that. Listen to us. Listen to me. Listen to Madison. Listen to the woman who will be the love of your life and the partner in all the great things you hope to do."

Shepherd took in Jamelle's words. He closed his eyes. He tried to re-envision today and every day after. Maybe he did. He re-opened his eyes and said,

"You are right, Jamelle. You are right, Madison. Come, Cyur. Accept my apology and come to the fireplace."

But as I stepped forward, an invisible darkness crept into my chest. A shadowy, vengeful beast pulled at my insides. It wanted only to destroy.

Destroy everything.

# 15

# PORTALS

MADISON WAITED by the dining room table until I was next to her.

I did not tell her about the destructive force trying to twist into my body and mind. I was sure I could keep this force from detonating.

Madison grasped for my hand. I gave it to her though I knew this would enflame Shepherd further. We then crossed the room together towards the fireplace. Our magical host knew he had to maintain his composure despite his vision for this moment being altered with my presence. But he could not stop his pupils from rattling at the sight of Madison's hand clasped in mine.

. . .

THE DARK FORCE dug with more fury, more desperation, to take hold of me. It wanted to rip me to pieces. Or vanquish me into oblivion. Wipe my existence from this universe as if I was never here.

"MADISON..." I started. I needed to tell her. She needed to know before Shepherd opened the portal.

"No," Shepherd said, his lips now shaking along with his pupils, "You stand here, you hold her hand, but you cannot speak. Do you understand, *child?*"

WHEN MADISON CALLED me kid it felt endearing. As if I was family. First as part of the college paper family. And then, over the past twenty-four hours, as part of a new family. A family the two of us had created together. Maybe it would never be romantic. Maybe it was never meant to be romantic. But it was said with love a family should feel for one another.

But Shepherd did not call me child as a sign of endearment. He did so to diminish me. How could a person so powerful ever want to diminish those he assumed did not have the same strength?

. . .

SHEPHERD COULD NOT READ my thoughts. He assumed he could. He assumed a lot of things.

Shepherd said to me, "Before I turn on the cameras, I want to give you one more chance to go back to the kitchen. There you will be safe. I cannot protect you if you are so close to everything that must happen."

His words could not do what his actions had failed already. Madison squeezed my hand as she said, "Don't worry about him, Shepherd. He's here for me. You're here for the world. Show them what you can do. Show them how special you truly are." Then she reached out to Shepherd. He looked at her hand. Now it was him who didn't trust her. He didn't trust this warped version of his sacred vision.

He said, "It has to happen today. I cannot pretend I'm not a God any longer."

"Okay," Madison said, holding her hand aloft for him to take. She squeezed my hand tight again. This time not easing it as she prepared for all that was to happen.

SHEPHERD NODDED TOWARD THE CAMERAS. They all glowed on. To his watching audience, he said, "Hello, my friends..." The calmness he displayed yesterday and earlier today could not regain control of his body. He pressed on anyway, "...

today you will see more than I had planned... you will see magic. Miracles. You will see death..." He finally took Madison's hand into his. The three of us a physical chain. With his free hand, Shepard began carving light particles out of the space in front of the fireplace. "...as I have said, these lights you have seen me manifest are not conjured from nothing. I have been scraping against the fabric of our universe. Tearing at the barrier between our world and another."

He kept slicing his hand against the air. Faster, deeper. The light particles erupted now. Like a welder with a torch against metal. We slowly realized he was carving a shape.

A door.

The view of the fireplace slowly disappeared, replaced by a view into another room.

Another world.

It was a bedroom. A small bedroom. It was night in this room, contrasting sharply with the midday light from our own realm. In a twin bed with a white comforter a figure stirred.

Shepherd said, "Lily, it's time to wake up... your daughter is here."

The figure in this small bed in this small bedroom in this other world sat up. Two meters on the other side of the portal door. The figure was a woman. A young woman. A teenager. Far younger than Lily Pike at the time of her death. Yet we all knew it was her.

Especially Madison.

I looked to her. I had been distracted by the spectacle of Shepherd opening the portal. Her hold on my hand had not altered. I assumed she was fine. But now seeing her face, the tears in her eyes, the quiver of her chin, I had to ask, "Are you okay, Madison?"

But she did not hear me. Or did not want to. Instead she let go of my hand and reached out to her mother. Lily Pike scooted to the end of the bed.

Her mother said, "No, Madison... you can't come. It's not your time."

"You're so young, mom..."

Lily Pike felt at her cheeks, remembering she no longer had the 40 year-old face she left her last life with. "Oh. I know. I'm sorry. Some people arrive here younger. They say we need more time to grow. I'm eighteen now but I woke up here as a child. Five years-old yet with forty years of memories of my life there."

"Why?" Madison asked, her hand reaching out to the portal.

I LOOKED DOWN to Shepherd's grip on Madison. That's when I noticed the glow. Not the light particles still trickling off the edge of the portal door.

But a new light.

A glow.

A glow inside Madison.

A golden glow.

Fire if fire could grow inside us. And this fiery glow was spilling down from inside Madison's chest, down her arm, and into Shepherd. As if he was draining it from her. Stealing her fire.

LILY PIKE SAID, "Why did I need more time to grow? Because... I was a young soul. Young souls arrive young here. You're an old soul, Madison. You always could see and understand so much. Even at eight. How old are you now?"

"No, mom... why did you kill yourself? Why did you leave me?" Madison's reaching hand neared the portal's door. Inches more and she would be touching the Ghostworld.

"Oh, Madison..." Lily Pike started. "It was impulsive yet inevitable. I was broken inside. I did not know who I was. I did not know who I was supposed to be."

"You were supposed to be my mother..."

Lily Pike now cried her own tears. "You're right... you're right... but I couldn't see even that... " Lily backed away.

"Don't leave me again, mom..." Madison stepped

toward the portal. Her fingers breaking the door's boundary. Enveloped in a blue sheen. She flinched. In pain. But she tried to press forward anyway. I stepped next to her, hand around her waist. Holding her back. She looked at me. Her first instinct was she wanted to be free of my grasp. Free to jump through the portal and into her mother's arms. No matter the price. But that inclination faded the longer our eyes held one another. Even as her mother spoke her eyes remained in mine:

"Madison, you need to let me go. I've heard stories about people traveling from your world to ours. They're monster stories. Beings neither alive nor ghosts. I don't want you here. I want you there. I want you to grow old. Grow to one hundred. Have babies and grand babies. Let your old soul grow so old you don't even come here."

To me, she said, "I can't let go."

"Your mom needs you to let her go," I said.

"No..." Madison said to me, her face strained. "I can't let go of Shepherd's hand."

MY EYES LOOKED AGAIN to where their hands were clasped. The fiery glow transference from Madison to Shepherd had intensified. Her face turned gaunt, grey. He might be killing her. Worse, I feared he wanted to.

"Let her go," I said to him.

But he ignored me. Instead he said to the cameras and the others in the room: "You have all now seen what I can do. I can connect the living and the dead. I can save worlds. I can unite worlds. I thought any witnesses to my power would put all their faith in me. They would see what I saw and say, 'I will follow you, Shepherd. Show me the way'. So my vision for today had always been one of love and healing. But someone I trusted asked me to change my vision. To abandon *my* destiny. So now I realize that I cannot trust everyone to understand all I must do. Those I cannot trust, you cannot trust..." He raised his hand like an orchestra conductor.

Jamelle, Katarina, and Nikki braced. William muttered, "I knew it." With a flick of his free hand, all four were thrown violently backwards through the air, over the dining table, and hard against the back wall.

Madison's body weakened. Her knees failed her. I held her up, put myself between her and Shepherd. But I could not free her hand from his. Not unless —

"I'm sorry, Cyur..." Madison said to me. Her eyes still in mine. Connected. United. Like they had been today outside the coffee shop. "I'm so sorry, kid... I think we could..."

"Madison!" Lily yelled from the other side of the portal door. "Don't ever stop fighting!" Her teenage-aged mother then threw a book from her world into ours right at Shepherd's head. It hit his forehead. Cut him. A trickle of blood. This trickle shocked him. Then enraged him. And rage always distracts. Just enough that it allowed me to free Madison from his grip.

I hoisted her in my arms, raced toward the exit only to find a large man blocking our escape. He had a gun in his hand. I spun toward the patio door. A second large armed man blocked this exit.

They were the security detail in the Cadillac outside Quest College. But not Madison's father's. They had been sent by Shepherd. They were going to make sure Madison came to the farm yesterday. At gunpoint if necessary.

Jamelle, Nikki, Katarina, and William all circled behind me. I backed us all behind the dining table. Shepherd snapped his fingers, closing the portal door before Lily Pike could throw anything else. Then he stalked toward us.

The armed guards remained at the only exits, ensuring we were trapped inside here with an all powerful mad man who had decided we weren't the loyal disciples he had envisioned after all. And if we could not exist to serve him there was no reason for us to exist at all.

/////////////////

KC jumped out of her seat, pointed down at the manuscript pages, laughed, then yelled,

"Oh, COME ON, Cyur! You are WAY too smart to not have seen there was only one way for this to end!" She sat back down, cackled, under breath, then muttered a defeated, "If I had been there instead of Madison, maybe I could have warned you..."

THE FIERY GLOW that Shepherd drained from Madison seemed to build in his fingertips, in his eyes, like flames ready to incinerate us all.

Jamelle, Katarina, and Nikki begged him to calm. Begged him to spare us. William, exhausted, lifted a fallen chair, slumped down into it, resigned to his fate.

I put Madison's feet on the ground, whispered, "Get behind me with the others."

Instead she looped her arm through mine. "No. My best chance is by your side. And your best chance is by mine."


"SHEPHERD…" I said to the supernatural being storming toward us. "…you are angry with me. Not them. I disrupted your vision. I'm the one who derailed your destiny. Let them go. And then when it's just us two, you can unleash your pain and frustration on me alone."

"I am not frustrated! I am not in pain!" He whined. "I am not angry! I do not get angry!" He raged. "No, I made one mistake in assuming mortals would see what I am capable of and not question it. Never again. I thought I would be a God of only love! That was the mistake! Because all religions need a God to be feared!" He raised one hand — the dining table violently flew into the air above our heads. Would he crush us with it? "A God capable of wrath!" He raised his other hand— snapping the giant table above us in two. He twisted both halves downward so the jagged edges hovered only a meter from our heads. Maybe he would impale us. "Only when a God's wrath is feared will a God's love be appreciated!"

With a brief bend of his wrist, he flung the two halves of the dining table with the speed of rockets out the windows behind him. The glass exploded. Nikki screamed. Madison whispered, "He's a lunatic."

Shepherd cried out, "No, Madison, I am a God with no more patience for mortal weakness! For mortal doubts! So all those watching online must see what happens when my followers disobey me... they must witness my wrath so that they can *earn* my love —" Shepherd pointed at the cameras. But at sight of them his face lost color. The record buttons were dark. He spun to Apple: "DID YOU TURN THEM OFF?!" With a single finger, ten meters away, he hoisted her off the ground, slamming her body into the ceiling. Before he could throw her across the room,

I said, "No, Shepherd. Don't hurt her. I did. I turned the cameras off."

He spun back toward me, seething. "Do you have some sort of remote control?"

I said nothing. Shepherd turned the cameras back on. "Witness my wrath!" He cried, his grip on who he was and what he was destined for disintegrating. But the cameras turned off before he could perform another act with powers poisoned by desperation.

He dropped Apple to the kitchen floor. She moaned in pain. After he turned on the cameras yet again, he turned his attention solely on me. The cameras went off a final time before he could take a step.

"Hand me whatever remote you have or I will kill you first!"

Madison said, "Give it to him, Cyur."

Nikki added, "If he's going to kill us, I'd prefer the world see what he truly is."

I had to say, "I can't... have the cameras on."

Shepherd raised his arms, thrust his ten fingers at me like a sorcerer set to unleash lightening. His powers tried to reach inside me — just like they had tried to do when Madison insisted I be by her side before the portal opening — but like before, his attempt to kill me with his magic failed. Venom boiled over inside him, bitterness for his failed dreams turned his face purple. If he could not kill me with magic, he would kill me with his bare hands. He charged the last steps between us. This superhuman, this self proclaimed god, perhaps capable of anything he could imagine, could only scream out, "I DON'T CARE THAT YOU DON'T WANT THE CAMERAS ON! YOU DON'T MATTER! YOU WILL NEVER MATTER! THOSE CAMERAS HAVE TO BE ON SO EVERYONE CAN SEE HOW IMPORTANT I AM!"

But a step before his hands could wrap around my neck, Shepherd froze in place. He was as shocked as the rest of the room. His security guards, guns raised, lunged forward. But they soon froze as well. Their guns dropping harmlessly to the ground before flying across the room and into the fire.

"What is happening..." Katarina muttered behind me.

I said nothing.

Shepherd, unable to move, vibrated from the inside. Every mortal and immortal desire within him could not free him. His eyes chewed into my face until they accepted what his brain could not. "You..." he managed to utter. "You..."

"What's he mean?" Jamelle asked from behind.

"You..." he said again.

"Look," I said. I pointed to his fingers. To his eyes. To his mouth. That glow he stole from Madison. That fiery glow. That magical light. It spilled out of his fingertips. From his lips. From his nose. From the corners of his eyes. It poured from him. Like blood might. Golden, glowing blood. But instead of dripping to the floor, it hovered in the air before flying into Madison. Fusing with her skin. Absorbing into her body. This fiery, glowing energy also flew into Jamelle, Nikki, Katarina, and William. And then, finally, even into Apple.

Each of them looked down as this magical essence entered their bodies. Crescendoing in them all with an orgasm-like finish before disappearing from our naked eyes.

The rage in Shepherd's body faded. All that was left was the broken heart of a man who thought he could only matter if he mattered to everyone. A single tear fell down his frozen cheek before the tension in him released. His body collapsed downward. I caught him before he hit the ground.

# 17

# THE MOMENTS AFTER

AS I LAID Shepherd on one of the couches, the unfrozen security guards raced out of the room and soon out of the house and, likely, off the farm.

Apple sat on the couch next to me and the unconscious Shepherd.

JAMELLE, Katarina, and Nikki paced around where the table once stood. Katarina was scrolling through her phone. "My assistant said the cameras saw none of it. A few seconds of his speech by the fireplace. But then nothing. Not the portal door. Not Madison's mom. Not throwing us across the room. None of his crazy stuff. None of it. No one will believe us..."

"But the cameras saw us levitating, right?" Nikki asked.

Jamelle said, "That looks like a visual effect on camera. I'm sure the collective response is that he's a fraud. That it was bullshit..."

"Jamelle's right," Katarina said, reading through the streaming comments. "Everyone thinks because they didn't see him open the portal that it was all a big fake."

"Should we go?" Nikki asked. "Shepherd might wake up."

Madison hovered between the table and the others. Looking down at Shepherd, she said, "Whatever Shepherd's powers were, I think they're gone."

"But how did he freeze? What stopped him?"

"Maybe," Madison said, "there's an invisible power protecting us after all." She laughed this off. But the possibility of its truth lingered.

Everyone besides William moved behind the couch and all of us watched as Shepherd's face and body softened, drained, re-formed, until the man on the couch no longer resembled the beautiful, brutal god from mere minutes ago. "That's him..." Apple whispered. "That's Henry..."

"Who's Henry?" Nikki asked.

"His non-hero name," Madison said.

"The light... that essence that left him..." Jamelle said. "That's what gave him his power. His beauty even."

"But that glowing energy left him and went into us," Katarina said.

"Shepherd was draining it from Madison to open the portal door," I noted.

"But that would mean Madison had the magic in her and Shepherd was just, I don't know, a magic vampire..." Nikki said.

William, still seated across the room, spoke for the first time, "All of us had it inside us. That's why we slept so well here. He was draining us while we slept. That's why he had to wait until today to do something as mind-blowing as open a door to the afterlife. He needed to steal our powers first."

"But I've never been able to do more than three push-ups let alone raise a turkey off a table or open a door to the afterlife!" Nikki laughed.

"Yet that glowing, magical energy knew to go back to you. And it's inside you. And I bet you feel normal again, don't you?" William said as he stood up.

No one could argue his point.

"None of that stuff went into you, Cyur," Madison said, her mind churning.

Jamelle said, "That's why he didn't want Cyur here. He had none of it inside him. Shepherd didn't want us to be his advisors. He didn't even need us to be his disciples. He just needed to steal the magic that was inside us... Feast on us whenever his powers ran low."

Katarina couldn't help but laugh. "Oh-my-god. This was like a science fiction film then it turned into a horror film and we were all gonna die... and now we are talking about how there's magic inside all of us I can't help but think this is some big joke. Like some crazy hidden camera show." She went to inspect the cameras. All remained off. "Never mind. But also. I need to go. Like right now."

"Wait, there's so much we just witnessed," Jamelle said.

"I know. I know. But no one's going to believe us even if we all swear what happened happened. We'll be jokes. Our careers will be jokes. I'll start a secret message chain and we can, I don't know, laugh about this in a day or a decade or something —"

"There will be more," William said.

"More what?" Nikki asked.

"More like Shepherd," Jamelle said. "William's right. This energy — this magic — that Shepherd stole didn't disappear. Someone else will figure out how to steal it and use it..."

"Maybe one of us will figure out how to use what's inside of us," Nikki said.

Katarina kept backing away toward the exit. "Like I said, this already feels like a crazy dream that I want to forget. If some new super magic person emerges, I guess we should assemble and go on CNN to warn people maybe... but until then, I need to pretend none of this happened." Katarina left.

William was next to step toward the door. "There will be more False Gods... and I am not alone in being determined to find each one, expose them, and destroy them until we find the one that created this simulation that we are all trapped inside." And with that, William, too, left.

Nikki said, "Now I'm feeling like I should go as well. Write all this down. Never share it with my editor. Never show anyone. But write it down."

"I'd like to read it," Jamelle said.

"Orrrrr..." Nikki said, "You could write it with me. I love your writing. I know I'm just an intern —"

"I'd love to write it with you," Jamelle said. A spark might have even ignited between the two. "And, like Katarina said, have it ready to publish the moment another Shepherd emerges."

Nikki and Jamelle gazed at each other. The possibilities of their connection extending in their minds with every breath. "I have a car," Nikki said. Jamelle grinned and followed her out.

"WELL," Madison said once it was just her, Apple, me, and the still unconscious Shepherd. "We can't leave Apple alone with him."

"No, we can't," I said.

Apple looked up. "So I have this... magic energy in me, right?"

"You saw it leave him and go into you," I reminded her.

She nodded. "He's been stealing it from me for years, hasn't he?"

"Yes," I said.

"He stole it from me. Made himself powerful and beautiful and then refused to be with me." Apple's eyes fixated on Shepherd's unconscious face.

"Oh..." Madison said. "We can't leave her alone with him not because he will hurt her but because she will hurt him."

"Apple," I said, "Madison's right. You need to leave the farm. You need to find somewhere safe you can be where Henry can't find you... and where you can't find Henry."

"I've built my whole life around him," she said.

Madison took Apple's hand in hers. Petted it like one would a frail elderly woman. "What did I say about all men being disposable?"

"Even ones that had magical powers?"

Madison looked at me, smiled, and said, "Especially ones with magical powers."

. . .

MADISON HELPED Apple pack up most of her things and walked her to the truck. I moved to the other couch, but remained with Shepherd in case he woke.

When Madison returned. I asked, "Do you think Apple will be able to stay away from him?"

"Doubtful. Us humans have a weakness for people that suck all our powers away and then abandon us." Madison poured two glasses of water, handed me one, and then sat next to me on the couch. Both of us facing the still unconscious Shepherd. She said,

"ARE we going to stay here until he wakes up because you want to make sure he's okay... or are we going to stay here until he wakes up so you can find out if he still knows what you're afraid he knows?"

//////////////////

KC mumbled, "Of course she knows, Cyur. You wanted her to know. Or maybe you only fall for girls you know eventually will."

18

TRUTHS

I TURNED TOWARD MADISON. Our eyes found each other and dove deep, into parts of ourselves we had held back until now.

She smiled, then, with the corners of her eyes holding back a lifetime of emotion, said, "I don't know if I should be more afraid you're going to kill me or you're going to kiss me."

My eyes could not contain tears long held in. I had so many thoughts. Thoughts I almost never shared. Even with the pages I write. But maybe it was time. "Madison... I only hide... this one truth... because..."

"It's okay, Cyur." She laughed. "Look! Now you have me jamming entire paragraphs into a single 'okay'."

I smiled. I loved that she could have a sense of humor even in a moment like this. "I... part of the reason I hide it... is because even though... you know... I love you... you think I would hurt you... I don't want anyone... not even someone like Shepherd... to be afraid of me. But you being afraid of me breaks my heart."

"You didn't want to come to Indiana to find a higher power to believe in, not really... you wanted to come here to find out if you weren't the only one."


I KNOW KC is going to show this book to other people. That is why I sent it to her. Maybe I want people to know that there are many like Shepherd who will use their powers — and steal other's powers — for twisted ends. Maybe I want them to know there also might be others like me. But mostly I want people to know that there is magic in everyone. And when they discover that magic in themselves, I want them to be ready for all of its promise and all its darkness.

So, to whoever is reading this, I'm sorry I'm only being honest about this now. I didn't hide it to deceive you. I hid it from you because I try to hide it from myself. I hide it from myself because I don't understand why I have these powers. And I don't want to use them until I do.

. . .

"CYUR?" Madison said to my silence.

"Yes?"

"Are you as powerful as Shepherd was?"

I tried not to react. Perhaps my lips flinched. But Madison knew.

"You're *more* powerful. To take away his magic, you'd have to have magic far greater than his." She paused. "You're going to hate me asking this — I mean, this might be worse than getting into bed with you last night — but can you show me? Show me how powerful?"

This did feel like a violation. Madison didn't understand how uncomfortable I was with it. She couldn't see the most important part of my condition: I hated it.

"You hate that I asked," she said as if she read my thoughts yet again. "I'm sorry... I guess I want to see why you hate that you have this gift... or maybe I needed to see some good magic after witnessing all of Shepherd's evil kind."

"I don't think Shepherd is evil... I don't think his magic is evil... I envied how sure he was of his reason for having his powers. I wanted to be near someone who could help me see why I had mine. But then it turned out Shepherd didn't understand why he was gifted magic any more than I did. But him being so sure that he was destined for power feels more dangerous than my being so unsure of why I have any at all."

"As someone who has been around privilege their entire life, no one understands why they were given money or influence or fame. Most people abuse their privilege. A few of the better ones use it to ease their guilt for having it. But no one understands why they have it. No one. Including me. Especially me. And maybe that's because there is no reason. It's totally random. If we admit to ourselves that the privileges we are born with were never earned or destined, our already fragile self worth shatters completely."

THAT'S when I finally understood the most profound reason I was drawn to Madison. There were a million ways in which we were different. But this unearned privilege — her money, her influence, her fame, my powers — felt like a burden, a crushing burden, that we had to understand fully before we even attempted to use them.

OKAY.

"Okay?" She said aloud.

*Okay.*

*Wait. You're not talking. I mean your lips aren't moving. And you just said okay.*

*And I just heard everything you thought.*

*Oh my goodness. This is extraordinary. I mean, this also makes me super —*

"Let's actually not do this," I said aloud.

"Because you could read *every* thought, couldn't you?"

"I stopped listening before you completed that last one."

"But you know what I thought..." She winked.

"I could guess. That's why I stopped."

"I'm flirting with you so hard, aren't I? Now I'm the dork with the humiliating crush and you're the cool, confident one..."

"Madison, I promise you I'm just as uncool and unconfident now as ever. When I look in your eyes, I feel so much longing, I have a hard time breathing."

"But you're... I mean... how can you not be sure of yourself? You're a god."

"I'm not a god. No more than you are."

"Oh," Madison said. "That glow... that essence... that Shepherd took from me... and then you put back..."

"I didn't put it back. I removed it from him, yes, but then it went back to you on its own. Everyone's magic is unique to them. So it all went back to the proper person from whom Shepherd stole it."

Madison looked down to her chest. Felt at her body. "Do you have more than me? More than others? Is that how you can use it?"

"I don't know. I don't think so. But I don't know."

"When did you first realize you could use magic?"

I hesitated.

"I'm sorry," Madison said, "I'm asking questions I shouldn't be asking."

"No. No. It's okay. I should answer this. I should be willing to answer everything. Maybe if I explained everything to you, you could help me understand what it all means."

"I'd like that."

I hesitated again until I realized what I wanted to say, "Madison... I could explain it... or I could show you..."

"Show me?"

I laid my palm open on the couch between us.

"If I take your hand, I'm going to see more than floating mashed potatoes, aren't I?"

I smiled as she interlaced her fingers with mine.

I TAKE MADISON TO A SMALL, white veterinarian's office. We stand in the corner. "Is that you?" she asks, pointing at the 12 year-old boy on the floor, holding my panting, exhausted dog with her bloated stomach hiding tumors no one looked for until it was too late.

The vet technician is on their knees on the other side of Flame. My mother has her hand on my back, rubbing small circles. Twelve year-old me is sobbing. I am begging. Begging her, God, the universe, anyone who will listen. *Don't take Flame away. Please please please don't take her away. Please please please.*

Madison tries to step forward. I pull her back. "Can they see us?" Then she covers her mouth, whispers, "Oh, crap... can they hear us?"

"No. But they can sense us if we get too close. And

we can disrupt, even disturb them, if we walk through their bodies."

"You've done this before?"

"Time travel? Yes. It's one of the few things I allow myself. But only because I've convinced myself I'm unnoticed if I keep enough distance."

"But you could, like, go kill Hitler when he was a baby or stop the invention of nuclear weapons or..."

"I would never."

"But, Cyur — you could save millions — and millions — and —"

"If I knew that was my role to play, I would. If I knew that's why I had these powers, I would. But I don't know. I don't know why I am the way I am and I will not use my powers to change history or — if I can help it — even the fall of a single leaf until I do."

The vet tech attaches the euthanasia injection. Twelve year-old me takes Flame's head in my hands. *I love you, I love you, I love you, I love you, I love you, I love you,* my younger self says. I cry. Now. Watching next to Madison. Tears fall. She squeezes my hand, pulls me next to her.

My younger self stops crying , but repeats over and over, *I love you, I love you, I love you, I love you, I love you, I love you, I love you...*

Flame's panting slows. Calm settles over her as life leaves her. And then it happens. That golden essence.

That fiery glow. It leaves Flame's body and flows into twelve year-old me.

I explain to Madison, "I could see it enter me. I could feel it enter me. Until today, when you and the others saw the magic flow back into you, I've never seen anyone notice it flow into or out of them besides when it happened to me at twelve."

"So," she starts, "You got your powers from your dog?"

I smile. I had never said that out loud before. "Maybe. Or she gave me hers. Or she made me aware of mine in a way that other people aren't. But as soon as I felt the power inside me, I knew I could do things — magical things — and I asked Flame, *Can I make you healthy again?* And she, like we were speaking earlier in our heads, said to me just as clearly, *No, my boy, no... this is my time to go... but you go see why you are. You go see why you are.*"

Madison says, "Your dog told you to 'go see why you are'?"

"She did."

"Well... wait, Cyur... your nickname you gave yourself..."

"Cyur," I say. "Spelled C-Y-U-R. See. Why. You. Are."

"So you never forget."

"So I never forget."

I watch Flame breath her last breath. Watch twelve year-old me keep telling her I love her. Then my mom turns me around and pulls me tight into her arms.

"That," I say, "was the last time my mother hugged me."

"Your mom died?" Madison asks.

I squeeze her hand.

WE TRAVEL to my childhood home. It's only hours after Flame died. My mom ordered pizza and soda. My favorite dinner. This was the first night it made me sick. Or my magic did. Or...

Madison and I are in the corner of the living room. My younger self and my mother are playing Monopoly while we eat.

Twelve year old me rolls the dice then says, *Want to see a trick Flame taught me, mom?*

*Sure*, she says.

I move my token — the dog — eight spaces. Not with my hand. But with my magic. The token floats an inch off the board and then flies just above it until I lay it down on Reading Railroad. The shock on my mom's face melts quickly into fear and panic. She stands up from the table. Backs away. *What did you do with my son*, she says, *what did you do with my son*, she repeats over and over.

"She got that upset from just you moving the Monopoly piece?" Madison asks.

"My mom knew it was more than that. My dad and older brother had moved out years earlier. It was just us. She knew me better than anyone. She could sense it. But I couldn't have guessed she would have been so afraid of me after that. She got religious. Fanatically religious. She would bring church leaders by, telling me to show them how I was possessed. But I never showed them. The more normal churches would kick my mother out so she would go to more and more extreme ones. They took her money and her sanity. I had to move in with my father within a year."

"I'm sorry, Cyur. That's heartbreaking. You lost your mother like I did, just to something different than death."

I nod. "This night, the night I showed my mother my powers, haunts me more than Flame dying. Because Flame asked me not to bring her back... but I feel like I should have known better than to show my mom my magic."

"You were twelve and you had been aware of these powers for not even a full day... there's no way you could have known. Your mother was the person you trusted more than anyone else. Very understandable you wanted to show her."

Madison squeezes my hand. She knows how to comfort me.

"So after your mother's reaction, you never showed anyone else your powers... until me?"


I TAKE Madison to my World Religion class. Sophomore year of high school. Fifteen year old me, in the front of the class, has my hand raised. The teacher reluctantly calls on me, tells me to make it quick. Fifteen year old me asks, each word painfully slow, *But... if... no... major... religion... has... been... founded... in... a... thousand... years... how... do... we... know... if... the... people... who... founded... those... religions... were... telling... the... truth... about... God... or... if... they... were... just... really... good... at... being... the... first... ones... to... sell... their... idea... of... who... or... what... God... might... be?*

David Kelly, sitting in the back, shouts, *Xavier, will you talk like a normal person for once you dork?* The class laughs. Even the teacher smiles. The only person who didn't was a sophomore girl in the back next to David. She has big eyes. Big hair. Striking beauty. Strong everything. She's at once, always, serene and fierce. When the room quiets, the girl says, *Cyur, I love your questions... you're the only one here actually thinking about what religion might mean instead of just memorizing rules and facts for a stupid test.*

"That's KC," Madison says.

"Yep. She was the first person to call me Cyur. Even before we dated."

"Listen, I get you really did date her... but she was WAY out of your league."

"Yep."

"But you became friends and you showed her your power and then she fell in love with you because, I get it, you're superhuman and superhuman powers are a turn on..."


I TAKE Madison to KC's basement. It's eight months after the moment in class. KC and my younger self are sitting on the couch. Our hands gently stroke each other even as our bodies cling to opposite ends.

*Cyur?* KC asks.

*Yes?*

*I love how you think about everything.*

*I love how you think about everything, too.*

*But sometimes I wonder if you think so much that it keeps you from doing other stuff.*

*Like what?*

*Like kissing me.*

*I just didn't know when the right time would be.*

*Now would be the right time.*

Our bodies lean, our lips touch.

Madison says, "I'm weirdly jealous."

When my younger self and KC pull apart from our kiss, KC says, *Can I show you something that will probably freak you out but also I think you might be the only person that won't freak out so I have to show you?*

My younger self nods. KC raises her finger into the air between us. She presses into it. Light particles form. Like Shepherd's. She then draws a heart with the light particles until it frames each of us from the other's point of view.

Madison says, "SHE knows magic? And she showed you hers first?"

"She knew how to do a little. I think her powers would have grown as strong as mine if I didn't show her what I could do." My younger self is so inspired by meeting another magical person, he leans through the light particle heart and kisses KC. Our bodies disappear.

"Where'd you go?"

"I took her to Paris. The Eiffel Tower. On the first day it opened in 1889."

"Now I'm really jealous."

. . .

SO I TAKE Madison to the top of the Eiffel Tower in 1889. I point to the faint shadows of my younger self and young KC through the crowd. KC's joy and wonder are exploding. She kisses me. More. Deeper. Jumping with excitement. My fifteen year-old self felt, for the first time since Flame died, that I might not be alone forever.

When I look toward Madison, the sight of KC and my younger self pains her. "How could you break up with her? She loved you before she knew you had power and then she has magic and loves you for your magic... you guys are soul mates..."

"I don't believe in soul mates, remember?"

I TAKE Madison to the soccer field outside Riverbend High School. We watch as seventeen year-old KC wins the game on a last second free kick. As her teammates celebrate, a cloud hangs over KC. After the game, Madison and I watch as seventeen year-old me tries to talk to KC. But a disconnection had been building for months. And this was the moment she broke it for good:

*Cyur, I don't feel like a normal person any more. Does me scoring that goal even matter? Should I be happy I made that goal? Did I even really make it?*

*Maybe you made it for me. Maybe you directed the ball into the goal...*

*I would never,* younger me says.

*I know, or I think I know... but I can't stop thinking that everyone else knows with certainty I made that goal on my own. That I should be happy. But I have to doubt it because of what I know you can do... Being with someone that can do anything makes me doubt whether I can do anything at all.*

Madison and I watch as KC walks away. Younger me staggers backwards in tiny steps as if shot by a bullet.

I explain, "Six months after college began, she wrote me a long letter. She had dated a bunch of men and women but couldn't stop thinking about me. She wanted me back. But I couldn't go back."

"Why? Because she slept with a few other people? Because you were hurt she had very understandable conflicted feelings about being with a super human?"

I NEXT TAKE Madison to a possible future. I am older. Twenty-five. KC and I are lying in bed. *I can't stay with you, Cyur... I can't... life doesn't feel real with you...*

Madison says, "You went into the future? Isn't that

against your rules of changing things? You saw the future ends badly with her so it altered your present day choices."

"When I travel into the future, I'm traveling into possibilities."

"How do you know they're just possibilities?" Madison asks but answers her own question. "You know because you know everything, don't you?"

"I don't know everything, Madison. And you're right, this was against my own rules. But when KC broke up with me, she broke my heart in a way I had not felt since Flame died, and I could not stop myself from going into these future possibilities to see if somehow, someway, we could find our way back together again. In every instance, KC ends up resenting me for keeping her from living a normal life. So going into future possibilities did alter my own present day choices. But I had never used my powers to alter a moment with others again until today. When I stopped Shepherd from hurting you."

Madison sits with what I said for a moment. "So, you've never gone into future possibilities of us?" Her gaze bores into my own.

"No. I've never gone into future possibilities of anyone or anything else. I didn't with Shepherd. I won't with you. And I never will."

Madison inhales a deep, long breath. "But I want to see our future. I want to see our possibilities. I want to believe in something, Cyur. What if you showing me the future allows me to finally believe life — and everything life makes us feel — truly means something?"

I TAKE MADISON TO A CABIN. We are on a porch overlooking a lake. The sun is setting over the treetops in the distance.

"Where is this? Our future?"

"This place doesn't exist. Or at least it doesn't exist in a way you and I could travel here without magic. I created it."

"What do you mean you created it?"

"I imagined it. I created my own lake and cabin and the world around it and as far as I know the only person from our world that can get here is me."

"How big is it?"

"I think it's about as big as earth."

"You think?"

. . .

I TAKE Madison into outer space to look at this new world from a distance. I say, "I think it looks about the same size as earth, right?"

For the first few seconds, Madison spins around space in gleeful amazement. "How are we up here? How can we float like this? How am I breathing?" Her glee turns to panic. "Oh, my god — how *am* I breathing? I'm not breathing, am I? *Oh-my-god* — " Her eyes close, her chest heaves —

QUICKLY, I take her back to the cabin. To the familiar sight of a sun setting over a lake. To our feet on a porch. To oxygen in our lungs.

"Sorry," I say. "I forget... You never could have gotten hurt. But that doesn't matter. You were afraid and I should have known better. I forget that I can do things without thinking through all the ramifications. That's why I almost never use my powers. So many things can go wrong." To help Madison calm, we sit down on the step of the porch, facing out toward the water. "I should have just found a book for you. I'm sure there are books written about how big this world is. Do you want me to find a book in this world written about this world?"

As her body settles back on solid ground, her mind

grasps for its own, "There are books here? Written by people? People you created?"

"Yes."

"Are there as many people here as there are in our world?"

"Maybe?"

"Do they exist when you're not here?"

"This world changes when I'm not here or not thinking of it, so I think so," I say. A dog starts barking in the distance.

Madison lets go of my hand for the first time since we started traveling. "I still don't understand. You created this place in your mind and now it's real? Or it's still just in your mind?"

"I don't know. See? I don't know a lot."

"But how can you not know whether this place is real?"

"It has become as real to me as Shepherd's farmhouse. As real to me as my dorm room at Quest College. It just didn't exist before I created it. Or at least I don't think it did."

Madison notices the barking dog down on the rocks near the lake's shoreline. "Is that Flame?"

"No."

"It looks like her."

"I know."

"Did you create that dog because you missed Flame?"

"Maybe subconsciously."

"Why did you create everything else here?"

"As my mom became more and more fanatical after Flame died, I felt an excruciating loneliness. So I created this cabin and this lake and a few friendly neighbors, one of whom had a friendly dog, to come visit. I felt safe here."

"You were just a lonely twelve year-old boy who created a world so he could feel safe and loved?"

"Yes, though I didn't really understand why I did until later. And then, the more I thought about what I could do with my powers, I thought maybe I should make this whole world very much like ours except one where no one felt unsafe or felt unloved. I thought after I made this world perfect then maybe I would have the confidence to change our world. So I made everyone here nice. And made sure everyone was happy. No one fought. No one doubted. No one felt unsafe. No one was lonely. But it didn't feel real. I could sense the people here hated not feeling real. This happiness I made them feel was a lie. It was inauthentic."

"And you value authenticity above all else."

"So I let go. Let everyone be free. Free to fight, free

to doubt, free to be imperfect, but free to be their authentic selves... and free not to be."

Madison touches the porch floorboards. Knocks on them to make sure they're actually there. She stands and steps down off the porch, puts her hand into the grass. She picks at it. "Cyur... time traveling to the past, imagining futures, reading my mind, taking away Shepherd's powers, even going to space... those felt... I don't know.... I guess I can wrap my head around those things. I don't know how to wrap my head around you creating an entirely new world... like this grass, your brain can create this grass, and then I can pluck it... am I plucking this piece of grass or are you?"

I do not respond.

Madison's mind twists from the piece of grass to my face. The reason I brought her here dawns slowly and heavily over her. "I'm feeling what KC felt..."

I do not respond.

"If you can create this other world, then maybe you created our world, too? And if you imagined our world just like you imagined this one, how do I know if the world I think is real is actually real?"

I do not respond.

"And if I don't know if my reality is real, how do I know if I'm real? If my feelings are real... if my feelings for you are real. If your feelings for me are real."

I do not respond.

Madison steps toward me. Takes my face in her hands. Her eyes again bore into my own. "And you don't either, do you?"

I do not respond.

"That's what haunts you. Even more than these powers you don't know what to do with. You don't know if any of it is real. This cabin and lake. Or Shepherd. Or your mom or KC or me or anything in our world in the past or the future... you fear it's all in your head... you don't even know if Flame is real or just a symbol of your power and your broken heart..."

My existential angst shook inside me yet Madison's hands grounded me. I said, "You see Madison. You see me. Whether I am real or not, or you are real, we see each other. And that has to mean something."

Madison points at the dog, then the sunset in the distance as she says, "Maybe there's a girl — not in our world, not in this one — but in a different world all together. And after she lost her dog — or lost her mom..." Madison pauses for a thought, then says, "Maybe then this girl discovered she had magic and then she used that magic to create our world so she wouldn't feel so lonely."

"I like that idea," I say.

"Can I kiss you?" she asks.

"Yes."

As our lips touch, all the powers within me, all the powers I had used, all the powers I had held back, still did not know whether any of this was real. But my magic wanted to believe it was real. So I let my magic believe. If only for a moment.

21

TIMES

WHEN I TOOK Madison back to Shepherd's farmhouse, I didn't know what was going to happen. Even if I did, I would have not changed a thing.

HE WAS WAITING, awake, a large knife held aloft. As we re-appeared, Shepherd plunged it into my chest. Through my heart. For a moment, I wondered if I could undo it. If I could stop it from happening. Or heal myself.

Madison screamed in shock, then screamed in anger. She leapt at Shepherd, trying to shove him off of me. But he had already let go and stumbled backwards. I grabbed his hand to steady him. *It's okay Madison,* I said to her without words, as I removed the knife from my chest. I bled like a human should bleed who had just been stabbed in the heart. This detail made me strangely satisfied.

As Shepherd realized he was successful in killing me, a terror took hold of him. Not unlike what my mother felt when she witnessed my magic for the first and only time. "No..." he said. "No... I didn't want to kill you... I just wanted to hurt you like you hurt me... No, Cyur... don't let yourself die..."

I held his hand and said, "Shepherd. It's okay. I took your powers, you took mine. I forgive you. Can you forgive me? Can you forgive yourself? Can you do that for both of us?"

He nodded. Or tried. Then stumbled away until he spun and ran out of the room. I fell backwards towards the couch. Madison leapt for me, trying to ease my fall. Then she climbed on top me, legs straddling my waist. Taking my head again in her hands, she kissed my cheeks. Over and over.

"It's okay," I said.

"No, it's not! Stop it! Heal yourself. I know you can. I know you can, Cyur! Heal yourself and be with me. I don't care if it's real. I only care if I can talk with you about whether it's real... that's *my* meaning of life. To talk to you about it... Our connection is real even if everything else isn't and that's worth living for."

I smiled. "That might be my favorite answer yet."

"So you'll heal yourself?" Madison held her breath as she waited for my answer.

"It's my time to go."

She sobbed, pressed her cheek into mine. "No, please, please, Cyur. It was too short. Take us back. Take us back to the car and make it a hundred hours. Take us to that motel room. Let's spend a lifetime there. A million lifetimes. Just the two of us. Just talking. Please."

"Okay," I said with a pained laugh.

"I can translate your 'okays' now. You won't do it. You're going to leave me. How can I find you? Tell me at least that. Will you go to the afterlife where my mother is? Can I find you there?"

"I don't know."

"Did you create the afterlife like you created the world with the cabin?"

"I don't know."

"How can you not know? You know everything!"

"I know so, so little. I did know I wanted to see if we could find love. And I think we could have, don't you?"

"We did," Madison said, tears pouring down her face. "We did. I love you, Cyur. I love you, I love you, I love you, I love you, I love you, I love you, I love you, I love you, I love..."

. . .

AS SHE REPEATED THOSE WORDS, I did what I had just promised I would never do: I travel into our possible future. To the first time Madison and I made love. To our first fight as a couple. To the white Labrador puppy we adopt. To her asking me to marry her. To our wedding day. To the birth of our daughter. To the birth of our son. To anniversaries, graduations, hospital visits, weddings of our children. The birth of our first grandchild. To Madison getting sick. *Promise me you won't heal me, Cyur.* I promise.

I see and experience all of this in a single breath. In and out. The joy. The pain. The fear. The love. The gift of a lifetime shared with someone. I want it all. I want to experience it all.


AS I COME BACK to Madison, bleeding, dying, on Shepherd's couch on a Thanksgiving afternoon, she sees I had visited our future. She sees all I saw. She wants it, too. She wants that possible future to be real, too.

Yet she knows to say, "It's okay."


AND IN THAT 'OKAY' she lived that lifetime with me.

And then she let it go so I could, too.

And then I died.

/////////////////

KC sat back from her desk. All the pages of Cyur's true yet unbelievable story spread out before her.

She knew what was coming. She couldn't travel through time like Cyur could, but she could sense things. The future. The possibilities. Not like Cyur could. Not yet anyway.

A knock at her apartment door. Then two more. KC didn't know what would be said or what could be said, but she knew who was there and why.

"Hello, Madison," KC said as she opened the door.

"How did you... how do you know..."

This too pretty, too sophisticated blonde woman asked.

KC said, "You believe all the things Cyur showed you and you can't believe his ex-girlfriend would know who you are?"

Madison started crying. KC knew she had to hug her. She hated that she had to. She hated that she needed the hug just as much as Madison. With their arms around each other, Madison said, "He's dead. He's gone..."

"I know," KC said.

"How could you know? He disappeared. His body disappeared. No one knows but me...

"Cyur sent me his book."

As KC walked toward her desk, Madison closed and locked the door despite being ten feet away. She had done it with but a tiny bend of her finger. When KC looked at her, Madison explained, "I can move things with just my mind. I think Cyur gave me some of his powers."

"He didn't give you anything," KC said and then, unable to hold back her competitive side, KC waved her hand, levitating two hundred manuscript pages off the desk. She flew them through the air until they were stacked together, hovering in a pile before both of them. The last page on top. KC explained, "Seeing what Cyur could do just made it impossible to not believe in your own powers."

Then KC pointed to the last page. Showed Madison how Cyur's book had allowed her to read about everything that happened since Wednesday. How she even read her own reaction to the book itself.

That's when Madison noticed what KC had known since the empty pages had first appeared: the words were typing themselves.

"Who's typing that?" Madison asked and as she asked the words 'Who's typing that' appeared on the last page in the exact same moment.

THE END

# AFTERWORD

*Good luck on your own search.*
*— Cyur Good*